CW00502331

G R JORDAN

The Slaughterhouse

A Highlands and Islands Detective Thriller Book 34

Carpetless

First published by Carpetless Publishing 2024

First edition

ISBN: 978-1-915562-90-6

This book was professionally typeset on Reedsy.
Find out more at reedsy.com

Film your murders like love scenes, and film your love scenes like murders

Alfred Hitchcock

Contents

Foreword

The events of this book, while based around real locations around Scotland, are entirely fictional and all characters do not represent any living or deceased person. All companies are fictitious representations. This book was filmed in Supermacleodation!

Acknowledgement

To Ken, Jean, Colin, Evelyn, John and Rosemary for your work in bringing this novel to completion, your time and effort is deeply appreciated.

Books by G R Jordan

The Highlands and Islands Detective series (Crime)

1. Water's Edge
2. The Bothy
3. The Horror Weekend
4. The Small Ferry
5. Dead at Third Man
6. The Pirate Club
7. A Personal Agenda
8. A Just Punishment
9. The Numerous Deaths of Santa Claus
10. Our Gated Community
11. The Satchel
12. Culhwch Alpha
13. Fair Market Value
14. The Coach Bomber
15. The Culling at Singing Sands
16. Where Justice Fails
17. The Cortado Club
18. Cleared to Die
19. Man Overboard!
20. Antisocial Behaviour
21. Rogues' Gallery
22. The Death of Macleod - Inferno Book 1

23. A Common Man - Inferno Book 2
24. A Sweeping Darkness - Inferno Book 3
25. Dormie 5
26. The First Minister - Past Mistakes Book 1
27. The Guilty Parties - Past Mistakes Book 2
28. Vengeance is Mine - Past Mistakes Book 3
29. Winter Slay Bells
30. Macleod's Cruise
31. Scrambled Eggs
32. The Esoteric Tear
33. A Rock 'n' Roll Murder
34. The Slaughterhouse
35. Boomtown

Kirsten Stewart Thrillers (Thriller)

1. A Shot at Democracy
2. The Hunted Child
3. The Express Wishes of Mr MacIver
4. The Nationalist Express
5. The Hunt for 'Red Anna'
6. The Execution of Celebrity
7. The Man Everyone Wanted
8. Busman's Holiday
9. A Personal Favour
10. Infiltrator
11. Implosion
12. Traitor

Jac Moonshine Thrillers

1. Jac's Revenge
2. Jac for the People
3. Jac the Pariah

Siobhan Duffy Mysteries

1. A Giant Killing
2. Death of the Witch
3. The Bloodied Hands
4. A Hermit's Death

The Contessa Munroe Mysteries (Cozy Mystery)

1. Corpse Reviver
2. Frostbite
3. Cobra's Fang

The Patrick Smythe Series (Crime)

1. The Disappearance of Russell Hadleigh
2. The Graves of Calgary Bay
3. The Fairy Pools Gathering

Austerley & Kirkgordon Series (Fantasy)

1. Crescendo!
2. The Darkness at Dillingham
3. Dagon's Revenge
4. Ship of Doom

Supernatural and Elder Threat Assessment Agency (SETAA) Series (Fantasy)

1. Scarlett O'Meara: Beastmaster

Island Adventures Series (Cosy Fantasy Adventure)

1. Surface Tensions

Dark Wen Series (Horror Fantasy)

1. The Blasphemous Welcome
2. The Demon's Chalice

Chapter 01

Clarissa Urquhart parked the small green car and jumped out, walking round to the far side to put her arm through Frank's. It was time to go out together, time to put away business for the day. For far too long, she'd come home to empty houses. She'd sat with her glass of wine alone, but now with Frank she had evenings to look forward to.

Not that every evening had to be something special. In fact, tonight, she was going to see a film she'd seen many times. An old black-and-white, a classic in some senses, and one that touched the soul in a good way. It would be bright and cheery. There'd be the odd musical number with it as well and that old-fashioned dancing. But above all, it would be time to just sit together and relax.

The cinema they were entering was a heavily restored building. Approximately three years ago, it had been finished, and the public were allowed back in after what had seemed an age. But Clarissa had seen an incredible renovation and for that, she loved the place.

At this cinema, you could get a drink at the bar. The seats were the old-fashioned kind, close in together, and you could disappear up onto the back row happily. There was one screen, that was it. One choice of film to go to.

She remembered when her parents had told her about going to this type of cinema and seeing film after film, after film, but all on one screen. There was even a newsreel.

Very different from today's cinemas. The large drink holder beside you, your popcorn on one side, costing more than a small island in the Caribbean. And seats that were so big and reclined that you felt like you were on a long-haul flight in first class.

The seats in this cinema would be smaller, but at least you could cuddle up. That was the trouble with these big seats. They were made for one. Everything was made for one nowadays, wasn't it? What do you want? How do you want it? That's what the modern day promised.

Clarissa reckoned that meant that you missed out on being together, being a part of something with somebody else. They were also good about mobiles in this place. If you had a phone out, they jumped on you. They didn't do phones here. Mobiles were for when you were outside. And you certainly didn't bring one out during the film where you'd be escorted outside to use your phone.

'What are we going to have before we sit down?' asked Frank.

Clarissa listened, thought for a moment, and then smiled at him.

'You have what you want. I'm going to drive back.'

'You can have a drink if you want to. I'll take the car. I am insured on it.'

'Yes, I know you're insured on it, Frank, but it's okay. I'll drive it.'

'You treat that car like it's some sort of—a baby,' said Frank.

'No harm to you, love,' said Clarissa, 'but that car is special. It is mine and as much as I trust you with my life, I wouldn't want you to damage the car. It could cause a bit of a problem between us.'

'Fine,' said Frank. 'I'll get a pint then.'

They walked in through the front door of the building, which was large and set in picturesque grounds towards the centre of Inverness. The river wasn't far away, and Clarissa could just about hear it rushing. The building had a slightly more modern exterior at the front, added with planning permission.

Clarissa thought it probably did the building justice. She wasn't for changing old things. She liked them preserved, kept the way they were, but sometimes you had to go with the flow. What was the point of having something old if it just did nothing? This was now a working building again. A place that people could come to. A place for them to share. It was good.

'Decent turnout tonight,' said Frank as they walked in. 'Plenty of vehicles in the car park.'

'I love this film,' said Clarissa. 'It's that bit in the middle. It always gets me.'

'In what way?'

It was the first time they would see it together. Frank remembered it from long ago, but it was one of Clarissa's favourites, and she had been begging him to come and see it with her.

'I might shed a tear.'

Frank made a motion as if he was about to fall over and she punched him on the arm. 'Don't be like that,' she said. 'It does. It's a cracking piece of cinema.'

'I'll wait and see,' said Frank. 'Anyway, I'm going to get to the bar and get my pint. Do you want anything else?'

'Get me a hot chocolate,' she said. 'But only if they do it right. I don't want just some packet and hot water. I want—'

'I know what you'll want,' said Frank. 'I'll sort it—don't worry.'

Watching him, Clarissa felt happy. Work was on her mind, though. She'd been moved up in the arts team and was now the detective inspector. Now she was calling the shots. She'd been impressed with Macleod, her boss, for he kept moving aside, letting her run the team. She never thought he could do that.

Seoras had always been full on when he had been the boss, the detective inspector. He'd been the one driving investigations. Now he was stepping aside, but he was controlling differently, in a way she liked.

Frank returned from the bar and handed Clarissa a cardboard cup, complete with hot chocolate and a veggie-ware lid.

'Let's go in,' he said. 'Come on.'

He put his arm out and Clarissa took it again and together they marched in, finding the row right at the back. They sat down in their seats. Clarissa leaned across, placing her head on Frank's shoulder.

'This is nice,' she said. Glancing around, she could see that most of the people in the cinema were older. But there were a few younger faces. She leaned over and kissed Frank on the cheek.

'Just so I know,' he said, 'are you expecting to watch the film? Or are you expecting some tender moments during it?'

'Tender moments?' queried Clarissa.

'Well, you know, you know what I mean. I don't know if you were expecting a—'

'A what?' asked Clarissa.

'You know,' said Frank.

'A snog?' said Clarissa.

'Well yeah, like a snog.'

'Frank, you are hilarious,' said Clarissa. 'If I want the snog, don't worry, you'll know about it.' He gave a slightly worried look. 'Don't give me that,' she said. 'You love it. You love it when I get all amorous.'

He put his arm around her, pulling her close, and kissed her on the top of the head. 'You know I do,' he said.

They pulled each other close, waiting for the film to start. The lights went down and trailers ran, advertising various products that Clarissa couldn't care less about. She noticed Frank got a little agitated.

'What's the matter?' she said.

'Can you smell something?' asked Frank.

'Smell something? I don't think so.'

There was a 'shush' further along the row. Clarissa tried to peer along and see who was giving her the evil eye. An older woman looked back at her, and Clarissa ducked back in at the ferocity of the eyes.

'Okay, Frank,' she whispered. 'What smell?'

'It's like rotten eggs,' he said.

'Oh, that's the stale air.' And then she smelled it. Frank was right, and it was becoming more pungent.

'That's disgusting,' said Frank. 'That smells like eggs, doesn't it? Like eggs that are off. Not good eggs. Not nice eggs.'

Clarissa sniffed again. She was getting it now. It really was awful.

'Oh, that's desperate,' he said. 'That's desperate. I can't believe that.'

'Why are there eggs in here? Rotten eggs?' asked Clarissa. She looked around and saw that some of the rest of the audience were getting anxious.

'That reminds me of a film I saw once,' said Frank.

'Rotten eggs remind you of a film. We don't smell things at films, Frank.'

'Of course we don't. But I remember it. There was a film back in the sixties. It was like a slasher. You know?'

'Don't watch that many slashers,' said Clarissa.

'Oh, this one was. I remember I watched it,' he said, 'because it had been banned previously. I was in my late teens when I got hold of it.'

'A banned film? What was it banned for?'

'I can't remember,' said Frank. 'I think there was just a lot of stuff in it.'

'Like what? Like guts and gore?'

'Guts and gore. Oh, a bit of nudity. Well, in fact, actually, a fair bit of nudity. And some coarse language.'

'Vulgar language in the sixties. I mean, how bad was it?'

'Actually, it was like a lot of films nowadays,' said Frank. 'The nudity wasn't that bad compared to some I've seen.'

'Well,' said Clarissa, 'I hope this smell goes away.'

'You'll get used to it,' said Frank. 'The nose does that.'

The ads kept running and Frank was right. The audience was slowly becoming accustomed to the scent—so much so that Clarissa began to not smell it.

'There we go,' said Clarissa, looking up at the screen that gave a rating for the film, and the signatures of those who had signed off on what rating it should have. 'Now don't talk during this,' said Clarissa. 'Talk about it afterwards.'

'Yes, your majesty,' said Frank. He received another punch in the arm.

'I mean it,' said Clarissa. 'I love this film.'

Frank pulled her close and together they watched the screen. Thirty seconds in, with the title credits still running, something fell from above.

It took Clarissa completely by surprise, when she saw the object descend at a rapid pace from the ceiling. The large object reached about five feet above the audience before a rope it was attached to went taut. Suddenly, the body was swinging back and forward just above everyone. For it was a body. Clarissa could see that now. And it didn't look like a live one.

Clarissa was up and out of her seat as the rest of the audience panicked. There was shock spreading throughout, causing gasps and moans while Clarissa tried to get underneath the point of descent.

'Everyone, stay calm. Everyone, keep calm,' she shouted. 'I'm Detective Inspector Clarissa Urquhart. Someone get me a knife. Can we get up there? Can we get up there?' She shouted, pointing up towards the ceiling.

Frank had got up out of his seat by this point and was coming across to help her.

Clarissa tried to reach up and grab the body, which was swinging, but she missed it. Beside her, Frank pushed down one of the flip seats from the cinema and told her to stand on it.

'I don't have the balance these days,' she said quietly to Frank. She stepped up on it. He reached up, grabbed her hips, and steadied her. The body swung past. Clarissa reached out, put her hand in front of it and got hold.

'Have we got a knife?' blurted Clarissa. 'I need a knife. You, over there,' she shouted at one usher. 'Get a knife,'

'Can you see his face?' asked Frank.

'No, his legs aren't moving. He might be unconscious,' said Clarissa. 'Someone, ambulance now. Ambulance and police.'

'What do I tell them?' came a shout.

'Where you are and that we've got somebody in extreme distress. Tell them it's being reported by Detective Inspector Urquhart.'

Clarissa was almost on tippy toes on the seat, her hands grasping the body that was swinging, but unable to reach any higher to pull it down.

'Let me do that,' said Frank. 'You organise people. Come on; that's what you're good at. Take charge.'

She stepped out of the way. Frank then leapt up onto the seat. He put two hands on the body, stopping it from moving.

'How's that ambulance doing?' asked Clarissa to the man she had barked at. And then she saw, running from the front of house, the usher holding a large knife.

'Frank,' she said. 'There's a knife coming. Can you see where to cut?'

'If I cut across the top, that should get him free. You're going to need to have people underneath to catch him.'

'I'm aware of that,' said Clarissa to herself, and turned round, detailing several larger men.

'How are we doing with my catchers?' asked Frank.

Clarissa then passed him up a knife. 'Don't cut it yet.' Quickly, she positioned men with their hands out.

'Let it go!' she shouted. With four men underneath, Clarissa told Frank to cut. It took him several minutes, but then the strapping that was holding the body up split, and the four men suddenly had the body descend upon them. One stumbled backwards and fell over, but the other three maintained a good catch. Clarissa told the catchers to lay the body down on the floor. She dived on top of it. But there was no sign of breathing. She checked for a pulse. There was nothing.

'I'm starting CPR,' she said. 'Somebody, go outside and direct the ambulance crew in here. Do we have a defib?'

'I'll get one!' shouted an usher.

Clarissa looked down at the body on the floor and she feared it was just that. A body. No life and soul. The defib later arrived and Clarissa worked on the figure, which she quickly identified as a woman. She used a knife to rip open the clothing, making her chest available, and placed the defib on it. But as hard as she tried, nothing was working. Ten minutes later, the ambulance crew came in, gently brushed her aside, and began their work. Clarissa turned and plodded away from the body.

She took a deep breath and felt Frank hug her. She sat down, taking a moment. It would all kick off again soon, whether or not the woman was dead. But for now, the ambulance crew were working and there was nothing for her to do.

Clarissa just stared down and suddenly a shiver ran through her. This was her night off. She wasn't on the murder team anymore. After CPR had been attempted, life extinct was pronounced. Clarissa had decided not to come back into the murder teams. She'd went to the arts team, but murder was seemingly going to follow her.

Interlude 1

The one thing I learnt from the movies was that you have to give it to them big. The opening act is a statement. It's something that says what you're about. So that's what is going to happen. Franz Kahn was a genius. The audience is all set for a happy film.

It's a date night. The girl is picked up and is brought to the cinema. It's a location that people feel comfortable with. They think there's going to be a romantic interlude. He's gentle with her, gives her attention. She happily goes with him. Instead of to the stalls, they go to an upper place, a place of quiet, a place of intimacy, and that's when it changes. That's when the film bares its teeth.

It's something that I learned from him. Whatever you do, lull them in early and hit them hard. It's time to hit them hard, very hard. It's a statement, it's the opening shot, and it's got to leave them flat out on the floor.

Chapter 02

Alan Ross sat on his living room floor, one hand holding a small toy car. He made a revving sound, mimicking an engine, before driving it up a large slope within the toy garage. He watched his son's little hands, working a wind-up lift, taking other cars further up.

Across from him, Angus was clearing away dinner plates. He had been late for dinner, as Ross had spent time in the office sorting out paperwork. He moaned to Angus about being a sergeant falling his way. But Angus told him it was teething trouble, and to sit down with his son and play.

Angus is good, thought Ross. *I'm lucky to have landed with someone like him.*

That being said, Ross was on call tonight, something he never liked. The trouble was, he could just be whisked away. He was now in a time that was precious because his son would go to bed soon. This was the time when Ross got to play with him. A time where they made their connection. A time that wasn't the weekend. For the weekend was a truly fun time as a family.

Working through the week, Ross was finding it hard to fit into a schedule that matched his son's needs. Not that his son was neglected. Angus more than made up for it, taking him here, there, and everywhere, but Ross wanted to be a part of that, too. At the moment, he felt he was falling short.

He moved the car across the top of the roof and found a little hand pushing it back. Clearly, it wasn't meant to go that way. And then another car rammed into it, causing Ross to laugh. He saw his little lad laugh as well, and then a smile shot across Ross's face. And in his pocket, he could feel the dreaded vibration. He was being paged.

Ross stood up, went to the house phone and placed a call in to the office.

'Sergeant Ross, sorry to bother you,' said the desk sergeant. 'Got a call to assemble. Out to Murray Court. I'm afraid there's been a killing.'

'I take it uniform are all there?'

'Yes, sir, we're on scene at the moment.'

'Have you spoken to Susan Cunningham at all?'

'Left that for you, sir, if that's who you want in. I think she's still missing her leg, isn't she?'

'I don't think it's coming back, Sergeant,' said Ross.

'No, of course not,' he said. 'Would you like me to call her?'

'No, I'll do it,' said Ross. 'Tell them on scene to expect me in about twenty-five minutes.'

'Very good, sir,' said the desk sergeant and hung up the phone.

Ross called Susan Cunningham immediately.

'Oh, hi,' she said. 'What's up?'

'Job,' said Ross. 'Are you up for it?'

'Of course I'm up for it,' she said. 'I'm back in and I'm not just doing the desk work. I've got my crutches; I can get about.'

'I'm just asking,' said Ross. 'I didn't mean to say you couldn't.'

'Well, everybody asks me. That's the thing, isn't it?' said Susan.

'I'll see you there. Or do you need a lift?'

'It's fine. I'll get a taxi in.'

One thing Susan couldn't do was drive a car at the moment. After saving the life of a young girl, Susan had been crushed underneath a falling building. Although she'd been pulled out of it by Perry and Hope, Susan's leg had been irreparably damaged and they'd had to remove it just below the knee. Ross had found her to be amazingly upbeat despite all that happened. But he wasn't sure that she was up to full speed. She said she was, though, and he'd have to take her at her word.

Ross kissed his son goodnight, threw his arms around Angus telling him he'd be home as soon as he could, and left believing he wouldn't see the house again for probably another twenty-four hours. It was the way it happened on the murder team. If this was a murder, they wouldn't see much of him for the next week or more.

The light was fading as Ross arrived at Murray Court. There were plenty of police cars about, and he could see uniformed officers taking statements. These would be the early ones, just to make sure that everybody had reported what they'd seen before they could be sent home.

As he parked the car, Ross looked over and saw a woman in a tartan shawl. He stepped out of the car, trying to focus in clearer. And then his heart half sank.

What on earth's Clarissa doing here? he wondered. *This is my case. This is mine to look after. She's not on this team anymore.* He turned and strode over towards her.

'How's the arts team involved in this one?' asked Ross.

'Just a minute, Als,' said Clarissa, and turned back to one of the uniformed sergeants. 'Now, have you got it all sorted? All the interviews done? Make sure we keep everybody out of there,' said Clarissa. 'Jona will be on scene soon. She's going to need to go through all of that.'

'Do you mind?' said Ross.

'Als, enough. I'll get to you in a second.' Clarissa turned and dished out some more orders before turning back to Ross.

'This is for the murder team. What are you doing here?'

'What I'm doing here is that I'm your number one witness,' said Clarissa. 'Do you want me to run through what's happened?'

'I should get the uniform sergeant to do that with me. He's the—'

'No. You've got a detective inspector right here who's seen it all. I've organised everybody. I'm happy to hand it over to you, Als.'

'What are you doing here, though?'

'I was having a quiet night at the cinema with Frank,' said Clarissa. 'He's over there. Poor man's in shock. He had to cut a body down.'

Ross shook his head. This was wrong. Frank was here as well. Frank was cutting down bodies. Clarissa was . . .

'Snap to it,' said Clarissa, clicking her fingers in front of Ross. 'Need to switch on. I'm going to give you the rundown before I go.'

'This is wrong,' said Ross. 'You shouldn't be here. You shouldn't—'

Clarissa looked left and right and saw some glances from some of the uniformed officers.

'If I could have a quick word with you.'

She didn't so much invite him to come with her as took his

arm and dragged him off to the far side of some cars. She then turned and squared up to him.

'Sergeant Ross,' said Clarissa. 'I don't know where the attitude's coming from, but I was here when the incident occurred. As such, I took charge of the scene. Uniform have arrived, and I was the senior officer there. I'm a detective inspector, Ross. You understand that? This is what I do. I don't care if I'm the arts team, or I'm in the lost flipper investigation team, or the dog unit. I'm the senior officer here so I've taken charge.

'If I need to hand it over to the murder team, that's fine, but at the moment, you're not paying me any attention. You're not in sound mind. Sort yourself out and I'll hand it over. If not, I'll wait for your boss to get here. Snap out of it, Als.'

Clarissa turned on her heel and marched off, heading back towards the uniformed sergeant. Ross scowled at her. He then looked over and saw a car pulling up. On the passenger side a pair of crutches emerged, and then Susan Cunningham half leapt out. She was in a pair of jeans, but which had one trouser leg cut halfway down. She looked over at Ross as she got out of the car.

'I'm here,' she said. 'Where are we at?'

Then he saw the driver's door open. 'What are you doing here?' Ross blurted. Perry stepped out.

'I drove Susan over,' said Perry. 'If you need a hand, I can give one.'

'I think we'll be fine. Everybody's here today,' said Ross. 'Susan, Clarissa's here. She saw the whole incident, and she's got charge at the moment. She needs to hand it over to me. Come with me, Susan.'

Susan hopped along behind Ross, and as he approached

Clarissa, he saw she was talking to Frank. The poor man looked dazed, a paramedic with him.

'Go with them,' said Clarissa. 'I'll be along just as soon as I can. You're in shock. You're okay, but you're in shock.'

'I don't understand. How does that happen?' Frank mused.

'Go with them, Frank, okay? Just try to relax. I'll talk about it when I get there.'

Clarissa turned round and looked at Ross with fearsome eyes. So much so that Susan Cunningham almost reacted.

'Nice to see you back, Susan,' said Clarissa. 'Are you—'

'Yes, I am. I'm ready and I'm fit to go.'

'Right then,' said Clarissa, 'come with me.'

She took them inside and stood at the entrance to the large room where the film was being shown. It was still running, although it was well towards the end now. Clarissa was pointing up at the ceiling, explaining how the body had descended, showing where Frank and she had been sitting. She also didn't step inside, worried about contaminating the scene.

'Any idea who the victim is?' asked Ross.

'Not got that far. Paramedics came, and couldn't get her resuscitated. I think she's been dead for a while. From my initial look, looks like she met her death by violence.'

'Why do you say that?' asked Susan.

'Just looks like she's been handled,' said Clarissa. 'But that's really just my opinion. You'll have to wait for Jona to get here. See what she says.'

'How do you get up there?' asked Susan, pointing up to the ceiling.

'There was a way around,' said Clarissa. 'The projectionist's office is up that way. You then keep climbing up into the gods.

I haven't been up but I've sealed it off for Jona to examine.'

'Good,' said Ross. 'That seems like you've got everything covered.'

'I have got it covered. I'm a detective inspector and I've been doing this for a long time. Okay?'

Susan Cunningham looked between the two of them, bemused as to what was going on. 'Is that rope stretchy?' asked Susan.

'There's not a lot of give in it,' said Clarissa. 'If you dropped her from the ceiling and you had a rope with a lot more give, you might actually have hit somebody on the way down before springing back up.'

'They'd have had to know, though,' said Susan. 'Know the height. There's a lot of planning in this.'

'Very much so.' Clarissa saw Ross looking back over his shoulder, almost with a look of disgust. She saw what the reason for it was; Perry entered the building.

'Anything else I can do,' said Perry, 'since I'm here.'

'Go home till you're called,' said Ross.

'Excuse me,' said Clarissa. 'It's still my scene.' She turned to Perry. 'You can do me a favour. You can start by making sure all the statements are collected. Make sure I've got a full list of everyone that was in this building. And then—'

'Sorry,' said Perry. 'The woman, the deceased woman.' He was pointing over towards the deceased woman. 'Can I get any closer?'

'No,' said Clarissa. 'We'll wait for Jona to come and then you can suit up and get all the way in. Why do you ask?'

'Look at it,' he said to Clarissa, 'look at the outfit.'

'What about it?'

'That's like more of a sixties' outfit, isn't it? I mean, seriously.

That's not an outfit people would wear today. I think I recognise that outfit too. I think I recognise this scene.'

'What do you mean, scene?' asked Ross indignantly. 'What are you babbling about?'

'That's enough,' said Clarissa. 'What are you seeing, Perry?'

'There's a film,' said Perry. 'I can't remember what you call it, but there's a girl in it at the start. She wears that sort of outfit, and she dies. It's an old slasher horror thing. It's in my mind for some reason,' said Perry. 'I can't think why.'

'Right, all of you out.' Jona had just entered the building, dressed up in one of her suits.

'Just coming. Haven't been in there,' said Clarissa. 'Haven't been up the top.'

'Thought this was a murder job,' said Jona.

'So did I,' said Ross. Clarissa shot him a look.

'I was on scene when it happened,' said Clarissa. 'So, I have charge until somebody takes it over. It is a murder, Jona, quite a clear one.'

'Fine,' said Jona. 'If you all get out of the way, we'll get cracked on. Is there anything I should know?'

'Body dropped from the ceiling on a large rope,' said Clarissa. 'Upstairs. I think there's something upstairs as well, beyond the projectionist room. That's where we think she was dropped from.'

'One usher said there were some clothes up there,' said Perry suddenly.

'Really?' said Clarissa. 'I haven't heard that.'

'Out,' said Jona. 'We can discuss all that outside as long as you've told me what I need.'

Together, everyone stepped out, and Clarissa turned back to Perry. 'What film is it? Do you know? Do you have any idea what the film is?'

'Let me have a think.'

'Have you contacted Hope?' asked Clarissa to Ross.

'I'm just here. The on-call's here.'

'Given what I've just been told,' said Clarissa, 'I'm not sure I should leave.'

'Come off it,' said Ross.

'I need to know what the film is. No idea, Perry?'

'I'll contact Hope,' said Ross. 'Bring her up to speed, see if she wants to come out, see if—'

'I'm going to wait,' said Clarissa. 'Please, go ahead with the investigation but I'll wait for Hope.'

'Why are you stopping?' asked Susan, as Ross walked off.

'I'm your number one witness. Frank also cut her down. Frank and I were in the building. It's probably best if somebody runs through it with me, so we get it all down on paper.'

'I could do that now with you,' said Perry.

'Cunningham, we got work to do,' shouted Ross from a distance.

'What the blazes is up with him,' said Clarissa. 'I tell you something, if I didn't know him well and somebody gave me the attitude he's been giving me, I'd give him a good skelp behind the ears.'

'He's not been right for a bit,' said Perry. 'Has he?'

'And you haven't known him that long,' said Clarissa. 'I've worked closely with him and he's not on full cylinders. That's the only reason I'm going to stay.'

'Well, I'd better get to it,' said Susan, hopping off after Ross.

'Right,' said Perry, taking out a pad of paper and a pen. 'Why don't we sit and talk through it—find out what you saw.'

Clarissa nodded. 'Are you sure about that film thing?' she said to Perry. 'You've seen that woman before?'

'I've seen the clothing before,' said Perry. 'I've seen the scene before. Can't remember what it was.'

'Okay. Then let's see what I remember.'

Chapter 03

Hope McGrath pulled up in her car and wondered what was about to confront her. Ross had been sketchy on the phone. In fact, he hadn't been himself. She had tried to check through what he had done but he kept muttering about not being allowed to do his role properly as Clarissa was on scene.

Hope always found Clarissa different, difficult even occasionally. But more from a manner of doing things, as opposed to any malicious intent. The strange thing was that Ross had always got on with her. Ross had even worked closely with Clarissa. It was a strange combination. Feisty, flamboyant, charismatic Clarissa against steady and highly professional Ross.

Hope first sought Ross and found him going through the interviews that the uniformed constables had made with those who had attended the cinema. He was quite belligerent in the way he spoke to her, and Hope told him to go ahead with it while she found Clarissa. It wasn't long before she spotted the tartan shawl. The woman looked tired, as if a weight was coming down on her. Hope didn't know what she'd been doing.

'Detective Inspector,' said Clarissa. 'At last, someone I can hand this over to.'

'I thought you quit our team,' said Hope, intending it as a bit of banter.

'Why, what's Ross been saying?'

'Nothing,' said Hope. 'I was just giving you a little dig. That was a bit of a strange reaction.'

'That's because he's been reacting strangely. Practically told me to go home,' said Clarissa. 'But I wasn't going anywhere. Not with what just happened here.'

'I got the gist of it, but fill me in on the detail,' said Hope. She sat down on the bonnet of a car beside Clarissa.

'I was out with Frank for a night at the cinema. We'd just got drinks and went through. Once we sat down, there was this smell. Absolute stink, like eggs. Rotten eggs. Frank noticed it much more than me. That lasted for a bit then people seemed to settle down. We'd had the ads, and the film had just started.

'This body just descends on the end of a rope. I mean, it unravelled. Stopped about five feet above us. I reacted,' said Clarissa. 'Jumped up. We eventually got a knife and cut the poor woman down. The paramedics came and worked on her, but she was gone. Upstairs, we think there's some clothing. Perry noticed that the clothing she's wearing is very 1960s, and he thinks that the whole scenario seems to play out to some sort of film.'

'No,' said Hope. 'Please, no. The ones who do that, it's like a fantasy. They have this sort of fantasy life, you know. Who knows what they're capable of?'

'I felt there's a statement being made because Perry said this looks like the start of a film he'd seen before. He can't remember the name. He's been taking down my statement, running through it with me, so we understand what I've seen. But I think you should be prepared for the worst.'

'Yeah, we'll need to jump on this, especially if it's a copycat of a film. And you say Perry hasn't got an idea what film it is.'

'Nope,' Clarissa said. 'He's trying, but it's not coming to him.'

'All that clever mind and he can't even remember the title of a film. That's depressing,' said Hope. And then gave a little laugh. 'Is Jona here yet?'

'She is. Inside. Probably best to get geared up before you talk to her. She gave me the rounds of the kitchen because I was inside when she arrived.'

'Oh, I'm sure you can handle her yourself. You didn't get to DI by being a wilting flower.'

'I'll hand it over to you then,' said Clarissa.

'Thank you,' said Hope. 'When were you intending to head off?'

'Soon,' she said, 'I really need to see Frank. But I kept an eye on Ross. He's not—'

'No, he's not,' said Hope. 'Macleod noticed it, too. He's not been right, but how's Susan getting on?'

'See for yourself.'

Clarissa pointed across to the far side of the building where Susan was bombing along on her crutches. She was talking to people here, there, and everywhere, organising the scene.

'She's quite resilient, isn't she?' said Hope.

'Takes a lot to come back,' said Clarissa. 'I'd be very careful with her, though. Just keep a very close eye. Sometimes it all looks sweetness and light and then it falls apart.'

'She was talking about a prosthetic. I hope she can get back to a similar mobility to what she had before.'

'Hello, boss,' said a voice behind Hope. She turned to see

Perry.

'You can call me Hope. You don't need to call me boss. I'm not Macleod.'

'I call him his highness,' said Perry, making a mock bow.

'Don't let him hear you say that.'

Clarissa laughed.

'Perry, what are you doing at the moment?' asked Hope.

'I was taking down Clarissa's statement, helping her get through that. I'm looking to see what else I need to do. Ross has got the scene, organising it. Well, apparently, I've turned up in a bad way.'

'Go find out who this woman is,' Hope said to Perry.

'Okay,' said Perry. 'Anything else? I'm on the phone.'

'I'm going to go upstairs. Have you been up yet?'

'No,' said Perry.

'Right, don't go too far. I'll take you upstairs with Jona. Might help you in working out who she is.' Susan Cunningham then arrived, hopping across. Hope saw the little smile she gave to Perry. He looked at her with a smile, but also a hint of concern.

'How are you doing?' asked Hope.

'I'm okay,' said Susan.

'Just make sure you are. If anything gets too much, you tell us. Okay? When you're ready, with everything. You don't have to rush back. You don't have to be here tonight.'

'This is what I do. This is where I am. I don't want to sit at home while everybody else is out doing stuff. I will not be a desk jockey,' said Susan.

'Nobody ever said you would be. Just until—'

'Until what? I get a prosthetic? Until we get this sorted? The brain still works. Most of the rest of the body still works. I'm just missing a bit. I'm good.'

'All right,' said Hope. Susan sped away on her crutches, and Hope looked at Perry. He gave a subtle shake of the head.

'She's not there with it yet. I think there's a lot inside. She's lost a leg. It's like losing a loved one,' said Perry. 'She hasn't grieved for it.'

'Stay close to her. Make sure if she needs help, she's taking it.'

'I will do,' said Perry. He walked off, and Clarissa gave a smile at Hope.

'What?' said Hope.

'You just told Perry to stay close. I don't think that's going to be an issue.'

'No,' said Hope, oblivious to the sentiment of the statement. 'Maybe it won't be. I'll be back,' she said.

Hope walked to the forensic wagon and suited herself up. She had looked for Jona, who was inside working, and who told her to take ten minutes, so she'd be ready for her. Hope found Perry and got him dressed similarly.

It was fifteen minutes later, when Jona took them up the stairs, towards the projectionist booth.

'The projection booth is in there. He heard nothing, as far as I understand. They're not actually in there the whole time. They simply get it up and running. It's not like the old days when they had to switch the films. It's a modern projector, even though it's an old-style building.'

Hope nodded. 'So what else is up here?'

'You go up into the gods beyond this. They've got the screen, but it's also got a theatre. So a lot of the ceiling has got gangways for the lighting and props.'

'Killer could have got away really quickly then,' said Hope.

'Drop the body, disappear. Nobody's spoken about anyone being up there.'

'Why would you?' said Perry. 'Your eyes would be on the fallen woman. Everyone rushing to get her help. He'd be gone. Down the stairs, come back inside, or disappear out the back.'

'So, it could really be anyone, then? Somebody from outside or somebody from inside. Great,' said Hope. 'I love it when we can narrow it down from the start.'

'This pile is what she probably arrived in,' said Jona, pointing at clothes on the floor. There were jeans, a jumper, a leather jacket.

'That doesn't look very sixties, does it?' said Perry. He also noticed there was brown underwear.

'Are you telling me, they've gone full detail. The body, it had underwear on, didn't it?' asked Hope.

'Yes, it did,' said Jona. 'It looks like she's been changed completely, which shows to me she's been incapacitated in some way, or else just killed. However, if you're going to dress someone after killing them, you have to do it quick, before the rigor mortis sets in.'

'You'd have to do it quick as well, because you're stuck up here in a building, and if anybody comes up, you are caught. You are bound to carry it out once started,' said Perry. 'A calculated gamble. Nobody's going to come up here, but if they do, you're stuffed.'

'Well, we need to check who was up here, if they saw anything,' said Hope.

'Will do,' said Perry.

'How was she killed?' asked Hope.

'Can't confirm yet,' said Jona. 'But from the look of it, she was killed up here. She was probably strangled, held. I'm not sure if she was injected with anything. I can't find any marks on the body at the moment, but I haven't gone over it with a fine-tooth comb yet. But she may have been asphyxiated.'

'Asphyxiated, dressed, tied up, and dumped. Why?'

'Well, like I say, it reminds me of a film,' said Perry.

'Then we need to see if that film is tied in,' said Hope. 'This is a statement. This woman hasn't been killed because of her,' said Hope. 'That's what it looks like. It looks like she was just somebody to die. The statement is dressing her up in sixties' clothes and dumping her down in front of a whole cinema.'

Hope heard her phone buzz, picked it up, and saw it was Macleod. She put her hand up and walked away from Perry and Jona, answering the call.

'I'm on scene at the moment. What's the matter? Not like you to call me. You usually wait for me to make the call to you.'

'Just had a local news man making the link between an old slasher film and the murder,' said Macleod. 'Have you seen anything similar?'

'Possibly,' said Hope. 'Perry thinks the whole thing could be a reenactment of a film he saw, but he doesn't know what the film is called.'

'*The Slaughterhouse* is the name I've got.'

'Okay,' said Hope. 'How old is it?'

'Didn't say,' said Macleod.

'Clarissa saw it all happen. She was the first to provide assistance. She's still here. Do you mind if I use her?'

'If she's okay with it,' said Macleod, 'but why are you needing the numbers?'

'Not the numbers. Expertise. Arts. Film is arts, isn't it? She might know that world better than I do. I was thinking I could send her off to find out about the film.'

'That's a smart idea,' said Macleod. 'That's a really smart idea. Yes, you can have her. I doubt I'm going to see her tomorrow, anyway, if this has happened. What was she doing there?'

'Date night with Frank, by the looks of it. He's pretty shaken up. Gone to the hospital for shock.'

'Then make sure she's okay with going and finding out about the film. I don't want to keep her back from Frank if he needs her.'

'Of course,' said Hope. 'According to Jona, our victim was murdered up in the gods, out of the way. I'm going to get Perry to find out about her. We need to trace who she is and make sure it's not actually anything to do with her. And it is about the film. That's where we're at for now.'

'Very good,' said Macleod. 'Keep me updated, okay? I'll not come out.'

'I'll talk to you at the station in the morning, then,' said Hope. She put the mobile phone away and turned to Jona. 'I need to see someone,' she said. 'Anything else you need to tell me?'

'Not yet. Still early days. Still working on most things. But it's a murder all right. It's not just a showpiece.'

Hope nodded and walked back down the steps, out of the building towards the car park. She saw Clarissa sitting on the car bonnet.

'I need to borrow you,' she said. 'Macleod said it was okay.'

'What if I say no?'

'You won't,' said Hope, 'but he said that's okay too.'

'What are you wanting?' asked Clarissa. 'I was going to see Frank if you're finished with me.'

'It's not a problem you can see Frank, but I also want you to find out about this film. It's called *The Slaughterhouse*, made in the sixties. I want every detail you can find on it. I take it that's part of the arts world. You would be au fait with stuff like that.'

'I'll get on it. I'll pull extras in if I need to,' she said.

'Thank you,' said Hope. 'Go and see Frank if he needs you, but if you can get this to me by the morning, I'll be really appreciative.'

'Okay,' said Clarissa. As she went to turn away, she paused. 'Is Als all right?' asked Clarissa.

'I don't think he is,' said Hope.

'Let's get him help. He's too good an officer not to be fully functioning.'

'Agreed. We are a little battered at the moment, though,' said Hope.

'Let's hope this case doesn't batter you anymore,' said Clarissa, walking away. Hope turned around, observing the building and everything on the outside. *Let's hope not,* she thought. *Let's really hope not.*

Interlude 2

The thing about a good slasher film is it isn't just about the killer. The killer's the mysterious bit. Our killer's the one people don't know who it is. They're forceful, they're bloody, too quick. The key thing is that they have to have something against them that people enjoy, people will root for. And when they root for them, make sure that those people get put under pressure.

You need a good detective, an excellent investigator, a talented private eye. Something like that. Can always have good opponents. That was the thing. People said it was all about the nudity or the violence, but what held the film together was those people on the other side. Those people you felt for as they struggled to solve it and then didn't solve it. It's key that those on the other side are worthy of capturing the public's best wishes.

That's why we do it up north. He's old school. He doesn't investigate much now, but he'll investigate this. They'll put him on it because it will go public. That's who I want. I want Macleod. Yeah? You understand that? Macleod's who we need. Macleod's the one that'll give a challenge.

He'll be uncomfortable in the public eye. But he'll also be thorough and determined. He'll relish being in the middle of the investigation and yet he'll tell everybody he hates it. The man's a champion. He's won before, several times. He's been on the news. They now wheel him out to cover up the other woman.

Press conference. Macleod says it, so that's okay. Not anymore. We're going to rip him apart. Rip them apart. That's why we go up there. That's why we base ourselves there. Why we do all of this. A great detective's what you need.

Only an outstanding detective can be brought down from such a height. Brought low. A pious man, a man of God against the evil. A man who doesn't shirk from his responsibilities. No shadow of turning with him. He wouldn't enjoy that blasphemy, but he'll be the perfect martyr at the end.

Chapter 04

It was the early hours of the morning when Hope called a team meeting on site. The Mobile Investigation Unit had been delivered to the car park at Murray Court, well inside of the holding perimeter that the uniform section was maintaining. Inside the unit, Hope was awaiting her fellow officers and poured herself some coffee from the side. It was thick and black, not the best she'd ever tasted, but at this hour of the morning she felt she really needed a pick-me-up.

She'd sent a text to Clarissa asking if she could attend. It was simply a courtesy, and nothing further. Hope knew she was asking a lot of the woman. She had been desperate to be with Frank and to make sure he was okay. Yet she'd done her job, as she always did, dealing with the situation first and foremost.

The first person to step into the room was Ross. He said nothing, but wandered over to the coffeepot, pouring himself one. He then turned and sat down without a word.

'All going okay, is it?' asked Hope.

'Of course,' he said.

'Good,' said Hope. 'I've called the team in, bringing Clarissa back as well.'

'I don't see the point. I know she was here when it happened, but she's part and parcel of it now. We should keep her out of it.'

'She is out of the main investigation, Alan,' said Hope. 'I'm not compromising that side of it. She's off looking into other things for me. The idea that this might be based on a film.'

'The rest of us could have done that.'

'That's enough,' said Hope. 'I know it's five in the morning, but that is enough. I don't need to explain my every action to you. There's enough going on without having to be grumpy about it. Whatever's up with you at the moment?'

'What's up with me? It's this—getting called out, then getting pulled.'

'Alan, we're not talking about this now. It's five in the morning. I've got a lot of tired people about to come in. We need to sit, and we need to focus and get on with what we're doing. That includes you and me. If you've got problems with the role, you need to come and talk to me separately from this.'

'I still don't see why she's in.'

'That is enough. Got it?'

The door opened and Perry held it open from the outside as Susan Cunningham stumbled her way in with her crutches. Hope stepped across and pulled her out a chair and held her crutches while she sat down.

'You okay?' Hope asked her.

'Tired? We're all right. I think we're just about covered everything.'

'Of course it's covered,' said Ross grumpily. Perry looked over at Hope, raising his eyebrows. She held her hand up, making sure that Ross didn't see.

'Anybody else for coffee?' asked Perry.

'I'll take one,' said Susan.

'Just made,' said Hope. Ross shook his head.

'Very good. When's the Highheidyin coming?' asked Perry.

'No, he doesn't do that anymore. Not at this hour of the morning. I'm seeing him later on,' said Hope. 'Clarissa's coming though. Should be here any minute.'

'I'll make up one then.'

Five minutes later, Clarissa marched in, pulled up a chair and flopped down on it.

'Good of you to have come,' said Ross.

'Don't start, Als, okay? Just don't start.' Perry placed a cup in front of Clarissa.

'Oh, you're a godsend, Perry. Anybody ever tell you that?'

'Just my mum,' said Perry. 'Not that often.'

'Well, you are. All right? And let nobody else say any different.'

'Right,' said Hope. 'Let's keep everybody on the go here. You're all tired; so am I. Let's find out what's going on. Ross, where you at?'

'I'm checking through the CCTV. We're trying to identify everyone in the vicinity. We've had everybody who was in the building do an interview. So, I've got names of all the cinema goers and addresses, looking through the CCTV and cross-referencing them all coming in. Also, making sure people weren't out of their seats for any period of time.'

'Do they have any of that technology scanning the cinema?' asked Clarissa. 'The ones with the check for mobile phones.'

'Not in here, no. That's not something they do.'

'Very good,' said Hope. 'I've got your list, anyway. They've got outside CCTV cameras; they'll help in the car park.'

'Yes, they have,' said Ross. 'And I'll be able to find out if anybody was there who isn't inside the building. I've also gone through all the workers who were on, who weren't on, and where they were.'

'Anybody out of place yet?'

'Give me a break,' said Ross. 'We're still going through that. Nothing glaringly obvious. There's only the one screen, thank goodness. Otherwise, it would be a lot harder to pin people down.'

'I doubt whoever did this is going to be a ticket holder. Nipped up past the projectionist. Were they up there?' asked Hope.

'No,' said Ross. 'Projectionist starts it and doesn't hang about. Wasn't up there.'

'Okay. We've got nobody upstairs except our two. Maybe he's taken her up there and pretended to be an amorous sod,' said Clarissa.

'We do know he killed up there, don't we?' said Perry.

As if on cue, Jona entered the unit and sat down on a seat.

'Sorry, we started without you. Wasn't sure if you'd make it or not,' said Hope.

'I have, and I'm here, and I can answer that question. Died up there. She was alive when she went in. Killed up there. Wrapped up and bound and dumped. Change of clothing as well.'

'Right, let's slow down a minute,' said Hope. 'So, our unknown woman is up there. The killer is obviously up with her and has killed her. And then dumped her. But we don't think we've got any of them on CCTV at the moment.'

'Not at the moment,' said Ross. 'I'm still going through it. Eliminating those who are on screen. Trying to find people who aren't. It's a lot of faces to go through.'

'That's fine, Alan. Wasn't expecting instant results.'

'All their statements are done,' said Susan. 'Everybody's gone home. When we find out who we want to talk to, we can bring them back in.'

'They got Frank's statement as well,' said Clarissa.

'Where is he? Did you get any time with him?'

'Not a lot,' said Clarissa. 'But he's okay. He's just in shock. He's coping.'

'Good. Hopefully, I won't detain you too much longer.'

'If I can go back to the woman,' said Jona, 'she was physically handled. I'm trying to see if I can get dental records and ID that way. But she has got markings on her wrists, across her face, chin, back. However, she's not been sexually assaulted. Looks like he's held her to strangle her, kill her, and then he's changed her.'

'That's unusual, isn't it?' said Perry. 'If clothing's removed, usually bodies would be interfered with. People would assault them earlier on, before they kill them.'

'That's often true,' said Jona.

'So, we can say the fact he dressed her in this way is important. It's a key part of this,' said Hope.

'Absolutely,' said Jona. 'He also changed the underwear.'

'Why,' said Perry. 'I mean, forgive me, listen. When she came tumbling down, and you were working on her, did you even clock the underwear? Did you sit and think, this is a sixties' bra, sixties' pair of pants?'

'No,' said Clarissa, 'although I had a dying woman on my hands.'

'Who saw her outfit?' asked Perry.

'Well, she came descending from the sky, Perry,' said Clarissa. 'Everybody was shrieking. We cut her down, and we did CPR on her. Right there in front of everybody in the cinema. Everyone saw her.'

'So, the description would get out. Papers will have it.'

'Absolutely,' said Clarissa. 'I don't think most people are going to clock that was a sixties outfit, though.'

'So what's it relating to?' asked Hope.

'Well, boss,' said Perry, 'like I said, I remember something. I remember an opening scene in a film like that.'

'Go on,' said Clarissa.

'Well,' said Perry, 'starts off with a girl being picked up by a bloke. They have a conversation. It's very lovey-dovey, down by the river, off to the cinema. He asks does she want to go up to the top and have a look. It's better than the back row. You think she's there to be—well, snogging and that.

'The film then continues until they're up and suddenly he grabs her in this room at the top of the cinema. He throttles her, grabs her wrists, all of that. And when he kills her, he then wraps her up and dumps her down in front of a cinema crowd. He doesn't change any clothing.'

'That's interesting,' said Clarissa. 'That's the start of a film called *The Slaughterhouse*. I've been working on it while I was down seeing Frank. *The Slaughterhouse* is a sixties' film. There's quite a lot to it and I need to catch up on it. I was planning on going home and watching it.'

'Once we leave the meeting, do that,' said Hope. 'I need to bring the boss up to speed soon. If you could come in on the morning meeting, that would help.' There was a tut came from Ross. 'Something the matter, Alan?'

'We can do that.'

'You have enough on your plate with the CCTV and you told me we're not all through it yet. There's a tonne of work to do. I'm not giving you a film to watch in the middle of that. Clarissa can do it. She's spare anyway at the moment.'

'Well, I'm not spare,' she said.

'Macleod said you were available to do this.'

'Yeah, well, he always says that, doesn't he?'

Perry grinned. 'What else do you know about *The Slaughterhouse*, though,' he asked.

'From looking it up, it was highly controversial at the time. Especially for its gratuitous violence, sex, and nudity. Didn't get past the censors, banned for a while, all this stuff. Compared to nowadays, it's probably pretty tame. But back in those days, it was deemed as horrific.'

'Anything else about it?' he asked.

'Very much. It's about to go on tour again.'

'What?' said Perry. 'On tour?'

'Anniversary. Sixty years or something like that.'

'They're going to run it in all the cinemas. It's reasonably well-known amongst entertainment news, but with this, and if this gets clocked as being a reproduction of it—'

'It's going to send it sky-high,' said Hope. 'People are going to want to watch it.'

'You think somebody's killed just to promote their film?' asked Perry.

'It's a possibility,' said Hope.

'Or could it be something else,' said Clarissa. 'Could somebody else in the film be hacked off about it coming back out?'

'I don't know. What I do know is that you need to watch it,' said Hope. 'Take some detailed notes. Give me a synopsis of the plot. Give me an idea of who dies when. All those sorts of things. You probably want to make a list of all the actors and the crew to see who's actually still alive. Sixty years.'

'Could be sixty-five. I can't remember the anniversary,' said

Clarissa.

'Do you think the people who made the film are still with us? Even if you're twenty then, you'd be eighty-five now. Some of these people will be dead. In fact, most will probably be dead,' said Hope.

'I'll get on it,' said Clarissa.

'As for the rest of us, a job to do. Back to work. See if you can get finished up in the next couple of hours. If you do, get a couple of hours' kip. I'm seeing the boss round about nine. And after that, I'll issue the next round of what we're doing. The plan remains the same. Perry, you find our murder victim, who she was, what she did. Susan is in here with Ross, keeping everything going here. Jona, get me a report on that body as soon as you can, and any other forensic we've got up there.'

'Going as fast as we can,' said Jona. 'I have photographs of the crime scene all loaded up onto the central system. You can show them to the man.'

'Will do,' said Hope. She thanked everybody for their time, and as they left the room, she kept Clarissa there.

'You need something else from me?' asked Clarissa.

'I just wanted to say thanks. Frank is okay, isn't he?'

'He's fine. He's just in shock. They're doing all the right things with him. He's going to have a rest. The worst is he'll suffer the odd nightmare stuff, but . . . maybe he'll understand a bit of why I got out of the murder team.'

'I think I might need you on this, okay?' said Hope. 'It's something I would have tasked Ross with, but he's not himself. I want to keep him on what he's good at. The sort of thing he can handle even with distraction.'

'Very good,' said Clarissa. 'Just monitor him. He's a good guy, Als. I think it's the kid. I think—'

'I don't think it's the kid at all. He misses Macleod. I think he was holed up with Macleod. He thought he was the bee's knees. Ross doesn't work with me the same, very different. I don't need mothering.'

'I hope you don't tell Seoras that—he needs mothering. He'd give you a dose of what for if you tell him he needs mothering.'

'You know what I mean. The man's a genius but he needs looked after. He needs everybody else charging around. Ross liked doing that chasing around for him. I don't need that. I need people providing inspiration, providing angles and theories. The grind I can do. I'm good at the grind. I'm solid.'

'You don't need a rottweiler either.'

'Susan's becoming one. I'll tell you that.'

'Yes, take care of her, too,' said Clarissa. 'Keep an eye. You don't get over that sort of thing easy.'

Chapter 05

Macleod knew he was going to be the freshest person in the room. He had coffee ordered from his secretary and delivered before Hope had even arrived. She said she was bringing Clarissa with her. Macleod wondered why. Yes, Clarissa had been there, but Hope would have covered all that off in a statement. Clarissa was directly involved in trying to help the deceased woman, but there was no reason for her to be part of the investigation. Still, it was Hope's investigation to run, and she had asked for Clarissa. So, Macleod felt it would be good to see what use she'd been putting Clarissa to.

There was a knock at the door, and Macleod knew who it was before the door opened. Without being told to come in, Clarissa appeared with a swish of the tartan shawl. It was rather abruptly whipped off and hung on his coatrack, almost making Macleod laugh.

'Do come in,' he said. 'I hope we haven't been inconveniencing you.'

'Quit it,' said Clarissa. 'All right! I'm doing you a favour here, so just quit it. I'm not meant to be up at this time of day, and I should be with Frank, anyway.'

'I heard he had a bit of a shock.'

'Afraid so. He'll be fine, Seoras. He's not used to this sort of thing. As I said to Hope, maybe now he'll understand why I got out of the murder team.'

'Indeed. And yet, here you are.'

'I'm only here because I've been asked to. And I've been up all night. So say nothing. You have a go at me, and I'll rip you apart.'

'I didn't believe that becoming a DI allowed you to become abusive to the DCI.'

'Only verbally,' said Clarissa. 'Is that coffee?'

Macleod raised his eyebrows. As if anything else would be allowed in his office. Clarissa poured herself one before he could even offer, and he watched her almost down it.

'Oh, that's hot,' she said. 'It's lovely, but it's hot.'

'Of course it's hot,' he said. 'Slow down.'

There was a rap at the door and a silence afterwards. 'Come in,' said Macleod.

The door opened and the tall, red-headed detective inspector strode in. Macleod could see bags under Hope's eyes, but her ponytail was neat, and she looked the part.

'Sorry I'm a touch late,' she said. 'I see Clarissa's already here.'

'If you want one, he hasn't poured one. The secretary thing's goes to his head.'

'The secretary thing does not go to my head,' said Macleod. 'You didn't wait for me to pour one. Give me that!'

'I'll pour Hope's.'

'I'll do it! She knows who she can count on.'

Macleod almost waved his hands in the air, making Hope laugh.

'Well, we're up and running, Seoras, but as you said last night, this may go very public,' said Hope.

'So, my guy's right. This is based around a film.'

Hope received her coffee from Clarissa and sat down, crossing one jeaned leg over the other.

'That's why Clarissa's here. We're on top of the scene. Ross is going through CCTV. We've got Jona covering all the forensic sides. We've got the photographs; they're up on the system at the moment, so you can look through them. Perry is trying to work out who our victim is. Ross and Cunningham are trying to narrow down who could actually have done it. There's a lot of spade work to do now, but what we know is, the manner in which it was carried out mimics a film, a film that Clarissa is here to tell you all about.'

'She's like, what, the police Barry Norman,' said Macleod.

Hope half looked at him, bemused.

'A film critic. Used to be on the telly. Gesticulated a lot. Quite good, though.' Macleod shook his head. *How did Hope not get that one? Surely, she's not that young.'*

'The film,' said Clarissa, 'is called *The Slaughterhouse*. It's a slasher from back in the sixties, only it was a real art-house thing. You'll love it, Seoras. Tons of nudity, tons of sex, tons of killing, blood everywhere, right, yucky, nasty stuff.'

'So why on earth is somebody trying to copy a film that was made over sixty years ago,' said Macleod.

'It's about to go on an anniversary run,' said Clarissa. 'Is somebody trying to boost the ratings?'

'They've not heard of advertising?' said Macleod.

'Apparently not,' said Hope. 'But there may be more to it than that.'

'Five murders in the picture,' said Clarissa. 'There are a lot of other things where there are attacks on the police who are investigating, but there's five actual killings. The first one, strangely enough, happens in a cinema. He kills a young girl he's amorous with, and then drops her down on a rope in front of the watching cinema crowd. That's exactly how it happened,' said Clarissa. 'I cut her down, but I couldn't save her. She was already dead.'

'Jona said she died upstairs in the cinema, so she walked in with him,' said Hope. 'I want to think that Ross can pull out some CCTV of her walking in with him. See if we can find our killer that way.

'I see,' said Macleod. 'But the murders go on. Clarissa, please.'

'Well, the second one is strange. Basically, somebody gets launched off a roof and lands in the street. Dies from the fall. But it's in front of a couple.'

'Right,' said Macleod. 'People watch this film—why?'

'Different reasons,' said Clarissa. 'Because it's what people did. For the nudity. For the gore. Who knows?'

'I was more of a summer holiday man,' said Macleod.

'No, you weren't,' said Clarissa. 'Probably didn't go to the cinema.'

'What's next?' asked Macleod.

'Circus act. Somebody killed during a circus act.'

'Okay. That's three. What else?'

'The fourth one's bizarre. It's a trap. The film's got several traps in it. But this one basically spikes two of the good guys. One dies.'

'Seriously,' said Macleod.

'That's worrying,' said Hope.

'Well, we'll need to make sure of what we do. We need to

make sure people stay safe when approaching scenes.'

'I'll give the instruction,' said Hope.

'What's the last one?' asked Macleod.

'You're going to love this,' said Clarissa. 'The last one is the death of the principal investigator.'

'How did they die?' asked Macleod.

'Decapitated by a mechanical device.'

Macleod stood up and walked over to the window. He stared out. It was bright enough now, coming towards summer, and the day was well underway.

'He doesn't like that view,' said Hope absent-mindedly to Clarissa.' Macleod overheard it but ignored the comment.

'Anything else you can tell me about the film?' ask Macleod.

'The killer taunts the local police,' said Clarissa. 'Sends in notes to the primary investigator.'

'You had anything?' asked Macleod.

'No,' said Hope. 'I checked the mail before I came up here, just in case anything had come through. No notes from anyone. I didn't get yesterday's. Wasn't in.'

'Okay,' said Macleod. 'So that side's not happening.'

'So maybe they're not following the whole of the plot. Maybe it's not a complete copy. Maybe they're just doing the killings,' said Clarissa.

'That's bad enough, isn't it?' said Hope.

'I'm thinking of the psyche. Why? I mean, the press doesn't need things to be done exactly the same,' said Macleod.

'One thing that strikes me about the film,' said Clarissa, 'a lot of the deaths were quite hard to stage back in the day, I would have thought.'

'What's your main line of attack?' asked Macleod, to Hope.

'CCTV. We should see him coming into the building.'

'True, but that doesn't always give you a clear picture. Other line of attack?'

'Identify our deceased. Got Perry on that. Find out who she is. Find out where she's been. Why is she with him? Did he kidnap her? Did she go with him willingly? If she went with him willingly, then find out who he was to her.'

'Good,' said Macleod. 'Let's see if Jona can back it up with any forensic evidence. I think you might also have to investigate the film.'

'How?' asked Hope. 'It's a film.'

'Talk to anyone that's still alive from it. I don't buy that somebody goes and kills people to hype up the film. Can you imagine if they found out you did it? It would destroy a picture house. Nobody's going to go for that. It's a grand scheme and one that can horribly backfire on you.'

'The film's got cult status anyway,' said Clarissa. 'I mean, this re-release—it'll do all right with it. They're starting with nothing, they've already got everything, they're going to book theatres, and they'll sell enough. The way the cinema works, it'll be enough; they'll make decent profit out of it. Not crazy profit, but good profit. That's why it's being put out there. This is not some sort of mega summer blockbuster.'

'There's also that risk,' said Macleod, 'that it could simply get banned if the police deem it a big enough issue. The film could get banned; censors could stop it if it was providing copycat killings.'

'Well' said Clarissa, 'I'm exhausted. I think I'm going to get some sleep. Then I'm off to see Frank. I'll try to copy over some of the stuff about the film, get some sleep, and then I'm off. I'll send you an email.'

'Is she good to go?' Macleod asked Hope, indicating Clarissa.

'Yes, but I want to stay. Can I sit here a moment?'

'You forgot,' said Clarissa. 'You want to tell me to have a day off for the time I've just put in.'

'I'd love to, but I can't afford to,' said Hope. 'Don't go too far. We may need you.'

Clarissa went to leave the room when there was a knock at the door. 'Come in,' said Macleod. His secretary entered.

'The morning mail,' she said.

Macleod grabbed it off her and began scanning through it. 'Thank you,' he said, letting the woman leave. As he scanned through it, he found a green envelope.

'The envelopes are described as bright green in the movie,' said Clarissa.

'Can't you see?' asked Macleod.

'Black-and-white movie.'

Macleod took the envelope and carefully opened it.

'What's it say?' asked Hope.

'Did you like my swing? It was hard to drop a friend. But that's the highs and lows of life.'

'He's got it wrong,' said Hope. 'He's sending it to you. You're not the primary investigator. I'm the SI here. He's got it wrong,' said Hope. 'He's sending it to you.'

Macleod simply held the letter in his hand and mused.

'That's right though, isn't it, Seoras? I'm the primary investigator.'

'Yes, you're the senior investigating officer,' said Macleod. 'It's on you. But he doesn't know that. Maybe he's just fired it in. What did the envelope say?' Macleod noted it was his name on the envelope.

'Maybe he just hasn't done the research,' said Clarissa. 'But I'll tell you now. This will also have made the press.'

Macleod shook his head. 'No, no, no. We're not doing the press. I've had enough of those people. I don't need a—'

'You're going to have to,' said Clarissa. 'That's the way this is going to pan out.'

'Probably need to address this,' said Hope. 'Get on the front foot with it; otherwise, we could get in a lot of trouble. You can get rings run round you media-wise these days.'

Macleod put the letter down, and then took a plastic bag and put the letter inside it, along with the envelope.

'You know she's going to turn around and tell you should have—'

'I opened it with a letter opener,' he said. 'I held the cloth on it. It shouldn't be contaminated, and she's got my prints. But if somebody's gone to this effort, he will not put his prints on it.'

'How do you explain that?' asked Hope.

Macleod's phone rang. He picked it up.

'Hello, Jim. Yes, Hope's just briefing me on it now. You want a briefing as well? Ten minutes. I'll be up to see you. Oh, and the rest of them,' said Macleod. He put the phone down and rubbed his chin thoughtfully.

'Are they asking for more?' asked Hope.

'Hope, get back on it. See if you can get me some results. It's good what you've all done so far. Let's see if we can pick something up. Something that says we're on top of this. This letter will worry them. This letter says there's somebody prepared to carry out whatever's in that film.'

Macleod waited for the women to leave and then he stood looking out the window. They were right; it wasn't the same view. But he wasn't watching anything that was outside. Instead, his brain was ticking.

Why? Why on earth would you do this? Though it had been a while since he'd been at the cinema, it certainly didn't get as exciting as this. He wondered about being called upstairs. That wasn't normal. They waited for half a day usually. Maybe the press was just going to go with this.

Macleod fired on the television and stood and watched as one of the national reporters talked about the death in the cinema. This was the start for Macleod. This wasn't somebody small minded. More like someone on a vendetta, keen to make sure the world understood. Who knew how far they'd go, or when they'd stop?

Chapter 06

Perry stood outside the police station over towards the smoking area. He was just a little distance from it. Two other colleagues were smoking but he stood upwind of them. His hands were in his pockets and every now and again he would turn around, looking one direction, and then the other. After a moment, he saw the little green sports car of Clarissa Urquhart pull up in the car park.

'Perry, what are you doing?' asked Clarissa. 'You out of cigarettes? I'm sure they'll lend you one.'

'I'm not smoking,' said Perry.

'So what? You out to get the fresh air? You out to show these other two smoking that it can be done?'

'I just need to get out,' said Perry. 'I've always just got out of the office for five minutes. Use to have a cigarette, but I'm not doing the cigarettes now. I told Cunningham I would not smoke.'

'You've always smoked, haven't you?'

'Yes, well, maybe I need to give them up.'

'Younger colleagues for you,' said Clarissa. 'Trust me, it doesn't help. They need to learn to cut the corn,' said Clarissa. 'Learners. But you and I need to learn to take the easy route, while they run off like mad, headless chickens.'

'Do you think the old clothes would still stink? Even now I'm not smoking?' asked Perry.

'What?' asked Clarissa.

'I've stopped smoking? Will my clothes still stink? Or will I be able to wash them and get it out? I don't know. I've never smelt my own clothes,' said Perry.

'As long as you wash them well enough to begin with.'

'But it's had years—years and years—of being smoked in.'

'Well, buy something new then,' said Clarissa. 'If you want, I can help you. I could give you some ideas of the sort of thing to get.'

Perry looked at Clarissa, a tartan shawl wrapped around her, the trews underneath.

'That's very kind,' he said, 'but I think I can find my own clothes. Bit expensive to change an entire wardrobe. But I might do it.'

'Why?' asked Clarissa. 'What's the big deal? Giving up the cigarettes and everything.'

'Cunningham said about them,' said Perry.

'So what? Cunningham says about them and you suddenly just stop.'

'Can I tell you something in confidence?' said Perry.

'I am the soul of discretion,' said Clarissa.

Perry looked at her. *An overtly colourful soul of discretion,* he thought.

'Thing is,' said Perry, 'I joined the team and, well, it took a bit to get involved with them, get them on side. Hope's fine, you know. I think me and her have an understanding now. Ross is tough work. But Cunningham, I just hit the ground running with Cunningham. She's got a rep like me, but like me, it's a rep that's not deserved. It's not like your reputation.'

'What do you mean by that?' said Clarissa.

'Tough nut. Doesn't take any nonsense. Happy to bust the rules and pile on.'

'That sounds good,' said Clarissa, smiling.

'Of course,' said Perry. 'They summarise it. They just say Rottweiler.' Clarissa's face went slightly darker. 'Well, I don't know,' said Perry. 'Cunningham suggests it, and I do it. What do you make of that?'

'That's just probably good for you,' said Clarissa. 'If she can get you off the cigs, maybe lose a bit of weight. She might be one of the best partners you've ever had.'

'You don't think I'm—'

'I don't do that sort of advice,' said Clarissa. She went to turn away, but Perry called her back.

'Something else,' he said, 'but about the case, the murdered woman . . . what did she do in the film?'

'In the film? She was a waitress,' said Clarissa. 'It was like one of those laundromats, or whatever you call them.'

'American, was it?' asked Perry.

'Made more for the American market. Not overtly British at all.'

'And yet we're getting it visited upon us here,' said Perry.

'A lot of Brits involved in the team making it. I think it was adapted to adjust to the American market.'

'Do you think it would extrapolate to finding a waitress? Do you think that he's copying the film that much?'

'I don't know,' said Clarissa. 'You got any other lines of enquiry for her? Anything else to chase down?'

'Putting the photographs out, but I'm guessing she hasn't got a criminal record. She's not coming up. We're going to get the DNA, dental records, but again, that's a heck of a hard trawl.'

'Well, give it a go then.'

An hour later, Perry had called all the local restaurants and cafes, asking about their female staff. There was no undue concern, but he found several women named who were not at work that day. He took down addresses and called them.

'I'm looking to speak to Anne McTavish.'

'This is Anne McTavish. Who's speaking?'

'Detectable Constable Perry. I'm just checking that you're okay.'

'I'm fine, thank you.'

'Just your employer said you weren't at work.'

'He did, did he? What's he got to do with it?'

'He's got nothing to do with it,' said Perry. 'I'm looking for a missing person. You're missing from work. You're at home. So, you're off my list. Thanks for your help.'

After another two calls, Perry had found two other women who clearly were taking a day off without telling the boss.

He telephoned another person, a woman named Orla, but got no reply on the phone. Perry told Hope he was off to follow up this lead and took his car out to a small estate on the edge of Inverness. It was an attractive enough area, and he found the house which had four flats within it, one of the more modern builds. He knocked on the door for the upstairs flat but got no reply. He stood for the next five minutes, thumping on it, until the door beside him opened.

'I don't think they're in,' said an older woman.

'Beginning to get that feeling,' said Perry.

'You wanting them for something?'

'I'm looking for Orla. Orla Burns.'

'You another one of those fancy men,' said the woman.

'I'm not a fancy man at all for any woman,' said Perry. He reached inside his jacket, took out his warrant card, and held it up. 'Detective Constable Perry. I'm looking for Orla, because I think she might be a missing woman.'

'Well, I haven't seen her. But there's that bloke that started coming round recently. I haven't seen her in a day or so.'

'The bloke?'

'Yes. I haven't seen him in a bit, either. To be honest, saw little of him. Passing figure. Never quite clocked him.'

'That's a pity,' said Perry. He reached inside his pocket and took out a photograph of the dead woman.

'I have to warn you, this might not be pleasant. I have a deceased woman in a photograph. It's not gory, but it is a deceased face. I was wondering if you could look and tell me if it's Orla or not. I appreciate it might be a shock.'

Perry slowly held the photograph up in front of the woman.

'Yeah, that's Orla. Did you say she was dead?'

'Unfortunately so,' said Perry. 'This is obviously her flat?'

'It is. What are you going to do? Kick the door in?'

'I was hoping to be a bit more subtle than that,' said Perry.

'Was going to say,' mused the woman, 'there's no need to kick the door in. I've got a key.'

'You do? Excellent.'

'Do you want to go in, then?'

'No,' said Perry. 'We're going to need the key, if you would, but I'm going to wait and get a forensic unit to come in. I would ask that you don't tell anyone about this. I'll inform the neighbours soon enough.'

Perry stepped back, taking out his phone, and saw the old woman watching him. 'I'll inform the neighbours soon enough.'

'Hello, is that Jona?'

'Perry,' said Jona. 'What's up? I'm up to my eyeballs.'

'I didn't think you had enough work,' said Perry, 'so I went and found you some more. Our missing woman; I found her home. I need you to come out and go through the place with me.'

'I'll be out shortly. Give me the address,' said Jona. 'It'll take me just a little while to sort out everybody else, make sure all the work's continuing. Seal the area off, and—'

'I know,' said Perry. 'Nobody's gone in. I haven't, and I've got a key, so you don't need to bring any lock picks, and we don't have to bust the place in.'

'Why can't we get more people like you, Perry?' said Jona. Perry laughed and closed down the call. He stood outside the front of the house, aware that the older woman was still watching him.

'It's going to be a while?' she asked.

'Well, these things take time. You've got to get the units together. I don't want to go in and contaminate a scene, especially if you've said that she's had a man in.'

'I'm not sure how long he stayed, or if he even stayed for long. She wasn't a recluse, but she was quite quiet, or at least she kept herself to herself. She had that waitressing job.'

'Was she fond of the cinema at all? Did she have any links to anyone?'

'Kept herself to herself. She liked her books. Maybe liked a little of the older cinema. I heard her talk about that,' said the old woman.

'Next of kin?'

'She's got a dad. He's in the funny farm.'

'Do you mean a mental institution?' asked Perry. He knew his hands were twitching.

'Yes, I do,' she said. 'Her mum's dead. I don't think she's got any siblings.'

Perry stepped from one foot to the other suddenly.

'Do you need the toilet?' the woman asked. 'If you need the toilet, you can use mine.'

'No,' said Perry. 'I'm off the cigs.'

'You should use those patches.'

'Maybe,' said Perry. 'You wouldn't have a coffee, would you?'

Half an hour later, Jona arrived to see Perry standing outside the door with a cup of coffee in his hand. It was his second one. Beside him was an older woman, talking away in his ear.

'Perry,' said Jona. 'Shall we go in and do an initial recce?'

'Of course.' He turned to the older woman, 'I've got to get suited up and do this, but thank you for the coffee.'

'You keep at it,' said the woman. 'Get off those cigs. Good thing to do.'

She stepped away, back into her house, casting a glance at Jona. A couple of minutes later, they were both suited up and opening the front door of Orla Burns's house.

Jona swung the door open into a bright hallway. There were pictures down either side of it, but none of people. Slowly, Jona made her way forward, opening the door that led up a staircase to the upper flat. At the landing, she opened the front door into a living room. It was small but neat. There was a two-person sofa, a television on the far side, a stereo unit, and a bookcase. Perry glanced across the variety of classic and modern titles.

'You approve, do you?'

'Well read, actually. And there're DVDs here, too.'

'So, she's into the old stuff.'

'Very much. These are old films.'

Together they walked round, finding that the woman had a taste that was certainly not from the modern day. Lots of older-style gadgets, including a tea's maid beside her bed.

'You see anything in here?' asked Jona in the bedroom. 'You want to check the drawers?'

'You happy for me to touch?' asked Perry.

Jona nodded, and Perry slowly removed the drawers. As he opened one, he saw a decoratively entitled book with the legend 'Journal'. He lifted it out and put it on to the side. Slowly he opened the book, coming to a date from a few days previous.

'Anything interesting?'

'Possibly,' said Perry. 'You go on; I'm just going to read this. I'll drop it back where it was. But I think this is coming in for evidence.'

The journal advised that she'd recently met a man. His name was Lucas. Perry wasn't sure if that would be his real name. She had met him a few times in coffee shops, although she didn't say which ones. He was interesting. Apparently, he knew a lot about cinema and had gone a few times. A later entry said she was going to see the cinema that night at Murray Court. He had popped round and had dropped off flowers, according to her notes.

'We've got a laptop here and a phone.'

'We'll take them in,' said Perry. 'I don't know if she's going to have his contacts. Can you—?'

'Get into the phone? Of course,' said Jona. She quickly was inside, using a pattern of entry. It was a lazy code, a simple square. 'I'm pulling up the photographs.'

Perry flicked through them but couldn't see anyone that

matched the description she had written of her lover, a younger man in his twenties. Most of her photographs were of animals or places like museums. Most weren't taken recently. Her contacts were minimal, too. Perry wasn't hopeful.

'Flowers,' said Perry. 'Dropped round flowers.'

'There's some in the living room. I'll check the bins,' said Jona. 'Although they might be in a vase, the wrapping might be in the bin.'

Perry began to itch and was struggling not to scratch himself. He walked across the flat and found Jona in the kitchen.

'Nothing with the flowers. The bin's empty. I'll get on and do a thorough search—see what else I can find.'

'I'm going to photograph the journal,' said Perry, 'then I'll leave it in there for you. Okay?'

It took Perry about twenty minutes to get a proper photograph of each of the pages. He replaced the journal where it had been and left the flat. Flowers, he wondered. He took a picture of the bouquet and the vase in the living room before getting back to his car. Picking up his phone, he called Hope.

'What is it, Perry?'

'Just done the initial recce through the home of Orla Burns, our murdered victim. I want to see if we can find anything out from her employer as well. But at the moment I know she was being visited by a man. I know he was bringing her flowers. So, whoever killed her by the looks of it, did a job on her. It's right in line with the film.'

'It was good thinking, Perry,' said Hope. 'Where are you going from here with it?'

'I'm going to follow your example and I'm going to go to the florists, armed with a picture of his most recent delivery of flowers. Might get a link to him that way. We haven't found anything in the house so far, except for a journal. But Jona's going to go through it with a fine-tooth comb.'

'Good. Let's hope she combs well,' said Hope. 'We need something. Waiting around in the dark. I know it's not unusual when we start up an investigation. We need somewhere to run, Perry. Four more murders. We need to be on this guy's trail as quick as we can.'

'Absolutely,' said Perry. 'I'm on it.'

He closed the call down, sat back and wound down his window, letting the air blow inside. He sniffed. Would he have to buy a new car to get rid of the smell, too? Was it seeped into the dashboard? On the windows? He wondered what it would feel like to not smell cigarette smoke. Surely there'd be a difference. Even if he was used to it.

He looked at the photo on his phone of the flowers. Time to work again. He thought about all the florist shops in Inverness. It could be a long day.

Chapter 07

Hope McGrath stood in her office going through the various interviews that had been done with the attendees at the cinema the night Orla Burns died. She was scanning through, trying to see if anything had been missed by her team. Hope didn't believe they had, but it was awkward at the moment, trying to find out who this woman was, who it was that had picked her up, who it was that had lured her.

Perry was out on the case, going through the one tangible piece of evidence they had, a bunch of flowers. Ross was still working through the CCTV, but he was struggling to find anything of use. Meanwhile, Cunningham was doing her best to keep everything going. Hope saw her hobbling round.

Part of her thought Susan should take time off after her trouble, but Hope understood Susan was a detective. She was an officer and, in truth, she didn't have that much in her home life. She'd just be sitting at home, moping about.

There was a sudden burst of activity within the main office and Hope turned to the main office door to see that Macleod had walked in. He made a beeline for her own office, knocking politely, entering when she told him to come in. He closed the door behind him.

'I've done something wrong,' said Hope. 'You've come in here like a bullet.'

'You've done nothing wrong, but I just met with some of the senior officers. The meeting I got called to, they're worried about this case. Anxious that it's going to go public. They think the media's going to take it over. They want it solved quickly.

'I've said to them, at the moment we're scrabbling about in the dark, because the person who's done this seems to have done it pretty well. We've not got a lot to tell them. They said they want me on the case.'

'Excuse me?' said Hope. 'I think we've made a pretty good start.'

'I think you've made a fine start,' said Macleod. 'But they want me on the case. They want the DCI's name up there, worried the public won't think we're taking it seriously, unless we put a DCI on it. They also are going to throw extra resources at us.'

'And what did you tell them?'

'I told them you were fine. I told them you could handle it. But they're not having it. And that's it, Hope, because they're the boss. What do you want me to do? Throw my toys out of the pram and storm out? It will not happen, because they will insist on this.'

'You're quite excited though to take over again, aren't you? To run something.'

'That's neither here nor there,' said Macleod. 'I've been instructed to do it. I need to do it. Put a call in. Get Clarissa to come here.'

'Clarissa? She'll be at home. I mean—she said at the meeting this morning, she'll have gone home, or she'll have gone off to—'

'No, she won't,' said Macleod. 'She might have gone to visit him, but she'll be back in.'

Hope turned and walked over to her desk, picking up the phone. She said a few words and then put it back down. 'So,' said Hope, 'You understand your other DCI better than me, but what do you want her for?'

'In a minute.' He sat down in the chair, then looked at Hope. 'Sorry, am I okay to—'

'Of course you're okay to sit,' said Hope. 'Now you're being polite, mega polite. Why?'

Macleod said nothing. Approximately a minute later, the door was knocked, and Hope told Clarissa to come in. She closed the door behind her and looked over at Macleod.

'What's happening?' asked Clarissa.

'I've been in a meeting this morning with the high hijons. Basically, they want me to take the case and run it.'

'That's nice,' said Clarissa. 'What are you telling me for? You want me to cover the arts section? You want me to make sure that—'

'No,' said Macleod. 'We're pulling the arts section in. They asked me to take over the case, so I told them, Hope's fine running the case but they insisted. So I told them I'm bringing the arts section in.'

'Why?' asked Clarissa.

'No. With all due respect,' Hope said, putting her hand up to Clarissa. 'I don't mean this in a nasty way. It's a murder. It's a damn murder!'

'It's a murder investigation that's got an art side to it. The film is going to be key to this, at the heart of it. With all due respect, Hope, you, me, Ross, we don't know films. We don't know this culture. Filmmakers, they don't behave like people off the street. They have a way of talking about each other. There's a process it goes through. The financial side, the publicity, all of that. Clarissa understands it. She understands the arts world, not just gemstones. She understands it all.'

'That I do,' said Clarissa. 'What do you want me to do?'

'We're going to run two lines of investigation, and I'm going to use my DIs to do it. Hope, you're by the book, you're solid, you chase up leads out of nothing. So, you're going to be doing that. You've got Perry, you've got Cunningham, you've got Ross. Go through the normal routes.

'Clarissa, you have the entire arts team at your disposal. I want you to research the film, its cast and crew. I want to know everyone who's still alive. Find me what went on with that film. I want to know about it being put back out and understand what happened with it the first time round. Is anybody annoyed, angered at it coming back out? I want to know if anybody is making money out of it. Or not making money out of it, when they should make money out of it. I want to know everything about it. Because at the moment, I don't understand the motive.'

'Of course,' said Clarissa. 'It's an anniversary tour. That could be at the heart of it.'

'Assume nothing,' said Macleod. 'It could be, but maybe not.'

'And you, Hope. You do what you've been doing. Where are we with that, anyway?'

'While you were out, Perry has found our murder victim—Orla Burns. Jona's in her flat at the moment, going through it with a fine-tooth comb. Perry found her journal, and it turns out she was being wooed by a man. He also took her flowers.

Basically, Perry's touring the flower shops.'

'Good,' said Macleod. 'Anything else?'

'Ross is having trouble. He has found no one untoward. He hasn't found Orla Burns on the CCTV either.'

'We're up against somebody good,' said Macleod. 'That's the thing. That's why I want you both.'

'Are you going to tell the team?' asked Hope.

'I'll tell them now. You can come and do it with me if you want. Might be an idea.'

'Something you've got to be aware of,' said Clarissa. 'I've said it before, but I'll say it again. In the film, there's a detective being chased around. They walk into several traps. He plays them and in the last scene, the main detective dies. If we're following the film—'

'If we're following the film,' said Macleod, 'that means he'll come after me.'

'Yes, given your celebrity status,' she said, holding up both hands and wiggling her fingers to make sure he understood, 'we need to be careful. The killer may have wanted you to be in charge. In this film, it's a male detective. He has a female working with him. She's not the lead investigator. Back in the sixties, that wouldn't have happened. The likes of Hope wouldn't have existed, or me. Not front and centre of a film.'

'No,' said Hope, 'we'd have been the candy on the side.'

'He's going to follow it to a point though, isn't he?' said Macleod. 'Does anybody else get hurt?'

'Only the murdered police officer.'

'Then it's two people every time we go into somewhere. What about Perry when he found the flat?'

'Waited for Jona,' said Hope. 'We are aware.'

'Look, I know you'll be angry at this. It wasn't my decision.

I'd have let you run with it. So, we get on. Okay? And it's the old team. You two know how to work together. And we work it like last time. Hope's my direct second, but Clarissa, you report in to me on the art side, obviously, sharing everything with Hope. Sharing everything, in fact, with the entire team.'

Clarissa nodded. 'I'll just tell Frank I'm going to have to disappear. Do a bit of travel.'

'And that's also why I wanted you closer in. I can't have you racing off here, there, and everywhere,' Macleod said to Hope. 'We're not that strong in numbers. Cunningham's, well, we'll have to see how she is. Ross, well, Ross is—'

'Ross is functioning,' said Hope. 'We will not solve whatever's bugging him quickly, but he's functioning.'

'Well, that's good,' said Macleod. 'I'm glad of that, at least. So, I'll pull you back together later on today. Let's see what Perry and Jona come up with, and we'll keep Ross on the CCTV. As for you, Clarissa, say your goodbyes to Frank. Tell me where you need to go, and I'll sign off the travel, but get me every detail about that film, and I mean every detail. Don't stand on ceremony—'

Hope laughed. Macleod turned to her. 'What?'

'You've told Clarissa to not stand on ceremony. When did Clarissa ever stand on ceremony? When did she ever not just get it done?'

'I'll have Patterson with me,' said Clarissa. 'I don't know if I'll need Ferguson. We'll see.' She stepped forward to Hope and put out her hand. Hope took it, a bit bemused, and shook it. 'It's good to be working with you again,' said Clarissa. 'Don't give the old man too hard a time.' Clarissa turned and went to leave the office but Macleod shouted after her.

'Hey!'

She turned back. 'Don't tell me you're getting annoyed because I called you the old man.'

'No. I don't need mollycoddled,' he said. 'You don't need to tell Hope to get off my back. She can do that herself.' Clarissa turned back to the door. 'And it'll be nothing like what the hell you'll give me,' said Macleod.

'Completely,' said Clarissa, leaving the office, the door swinging shut behind her.

'Shall we tell everyone?'

'Okay, Seoras,' said Hope. The pair left Hope's office and made a quick announcement with the team before Macleod phoned Perry to advise him of what was going on.

'Okay,' said Perry, 'but I'm still reporting directly to Hope at the moment. Is that right?'

'Yes, Perry. Where are you at?' asked Macleod.

'I am ready to buy a new pair of shoes,' he said. 'Seems to me that these florists are miles apart. I've still got plenty more to cover, but no luck so far.'

'What type of flowers are they?' asked Macleod.

'Yellow, and I think some are pink,' said Perry.

Macleod shook his head. 'Seriously?'

He said goodbye to Perry and then walked back up to the office. Macleod would have loved to have been back downstairs in amongst the team permanently. He could take over Hope's office, but it was hers. He needed to give her that respect, since she had the case whipped out from underneath her.

Macleod sat down in his seat, opened some files on the computer and began reading through them, making sure he was fully up to speed with what had happened. A cup of coffee appeared from his secretary, for which he thanked her, and he sat drinking it. As he turned away from the files, letting the information digest in his brain, he smiled. He picked up the phone and called his partner, Jane.

'You're phoning me in the middle of the day. What's wrong?'

'There's nothing wrong.'

'You've got a murdered girl. You've got the TV going crazy to tell the public, and apparently, you're phoning me in the middle of the day to tell me nothing's wrong. Don't lie to me, Seoras. What's going on?'

'They've asked me to take this case.'

'I thought it was yours, anyway. You run the murder teams, don't you?'

'No. Well, yes. It could be put out to a lot of different people. What I mean is, it's not just my department running it, not just my people. They want me to run it.'

Jane went quiet on the other end.

'Are you all right?' he asked.

'Are you?'

'Yes.'

'I guess I won't see you then, probably for a week or two. You think this could be a long one?'

'Who knows? I'll probably know soon enough, but I doubt I'll be home tonight. Sorry, I'll try to get home the night after. I'll have to see what's going on.'

'Don't apologise to me, Seoras. Just keep going, get home when you can, and go catch that killer.'

'I'm sorry about it,' he said.

'No, you're not. You're just saying what you think I want to hear. Seoras, you're not sorry. You're back in the saddle, the one running this. You're over the moon inside. I know you don't show it, Seoras, because that wouldn't be right, to show it when somebody's dead. But inside, your soul's feet are dancing!'

'You know me too well.'

He said goodbye and put the phone down. Macleod sat back in his chair. He was happy. The thrill and excitement were coming back. The chase was on already. He'd watched the last couple from the sidelines, forcibly kept himself back so as not to get in Hope's or Clarissa's way. But now, now the baton was his.

And more than that, he seemed to have an adversary who was trying to get the better of him, maybe even play games with him. Something inside of him, Macleod, relished this, even if he wasn't sure he should. He stood up from the table and went to make his way back downstairs. He needed to spend time in that room. That's where it all happened, not up in his office. Macleod descended the stairs.

Chapter 08

Perry kept on walking. Walking was keeping him from stopping and giving in to his restless hands. It was stopping him from trying to reach for a cigarette. He didn't have any on him, but he was passing enough newsagents and shops that he could soon pick up a packet.

Perry had made sure he left all his matches behind. He was giving himself every opportunity, and yet he was shaking. Maybe he should use those patches, but the idea of going cold turkey—the idea of that challenge—called to him.

Perry entered a flower shop in the middle of the city and was greeted with a bright smile by a woman in her mid-forties. She had auburn hair, and Perry thought her smile was delightful.

'How can I help you?' she asked. 'Are you looking for something for the wife?'

'I haven't got a wife,' said Perry. 'That's why I keep this incredibly sprightly and youthful figure.'

The woman laughed. 'What can I do for you?'

'My name's Detective Constable Perry. I'm looking to see if you sold these flowers.' He pulled out his phone and held up an image of the flowers in Orla Burns's house.

'Do you know the wrapping that they came in?' she asked,

'because, well, yeah, I could have sold those flowers. I'm not sure. They're just a load of flowers in a vase.'

'I thought you might know,' said Perry.

'I'm sorry,' she said; 'we do quite a lot here and there's other people wrapping up. If I saw the packaging, I could tell you it was ours. But then again, if you saw the packaging, you could probably tell it was ours, anyway. It's got our name all over it.'

'Okay,' said Perry. 'Thank you, though.'

He disappeared from the shop and trudged to the next one. The day soon blended into three shops later, and Perry was absolutely exhausted. He had walked and not kept going back to the car because it was easier within town. And now here he was, coming towards what was the last flower shop before having to take himself to the outskirts of the city.

'Hello, I'm Detective Constable Perry, and I'm here to ask if these are your flowers.'

Perry held up the photograph without even acknowledging the woman behind the counter, because of the fatigue in his feet.

'Yeah, those are ours,' she said.

Perry looked up. A blonde-haired woman stood with her arms folded, smiling back at him. She was of a large frame, and, in truth, Perry liked her. But he ignored himself and instead asked her the obvious question.

'How do you know those are yours?'

'Because that's the way I would arrange them. That's the way I would put them together. There are three different flowers. You might not be aware of that. Do you know anything about flowers?'

'Nothing at all,' said Perry. 'I just see the colours.'

'Those three go together. In fact, yes, I put those together, especially for a man who found out they were a woman's favourite flowers. Yes, yes, I've got him now,' she said. 'Used to come in with a hat on. Gravelly voice. Always got that feeling he just wasn't who he said he was. What am I like with my stories about the customers? He purchased from us several times. But he came and got this unique spray, and I don't think he's been back since. These were what—three, four days ago?'

'Do you know how he paid?' asked Perry.

'Yes, paid by cash.'

Perry almost swore. 'So,' said Perry, 'he comes in, pays you cash, and takes the flowers.'

'That's correct.'

'Did you get a name?'

'No,' she said. 'We didn't get a name, although once he struggled to get the flowers after work and we had to run round to his address.'

'How did you not get his name, then?'

'Well, the thing was, we were just having a conversation. He gave me the address and then by the time he left the shop, I suddenly thought, I don't have his name. But I had the address so I could still deliver them. And I had his cash since he paid up front for them.'

'So, where does he live?'

'Well, give me a moment,' said the woman. She flipped through an order book, eventually arriving at a specific date, and wrote down an address.

'Yes, that's it.'

'That's very kind of you,' said Perry. 'If I need some, I'll come back here and get some flowers off you. In fact, I might need some soon.'

'Really,' said the woman. 'Who would that be for?'

'Colleague,' said Perry. 'She's been very helpful.'

'And you wish to give her flowers?'

'Yeah,' said Perry. 'It's a nice thing to do without sounding too—'

'Too what?' asked the woman.

'Well, you can get flowers that aren't really romantic, can't you?'

'Flowers can be whatever you want them to be,' said the woman. 'I can make up a batch. Make them say whatever you want them to say.'

'Thanks,' said Perry. He left the flower shop and walked back to the car. Once inside, he placed a call back to the office. Susan Cunningham picked up.

'Susan, I need somebody out with me. I've got an address for our man. It's an address he had some flowers delivered to him. I need to check it out. You got Ross or Hope there?'

'I think they're busy, Perry. I'm not though. Ross hasn't let me get a word in. He dominates everything. Do you know that? I can understand why Patterson had problems with him.'

'But you're not allowed out and about? They were keeping you on the paperwork, weren't they?'

'He didn't say that to me. But it is difficult since I can't drive.'

'We need two to investigate,' said Perry. 'That was the rule. And I'm now going to a place that will not be public. I don't want to drag Jona off her work in case this isn't the right address. Why don't you come with me initially?'

'Very good,' she said. 'I'll get there, if you take me. I'll wait for you out in the car park.'

'Make sure you tell Hope where we're going.'

'Will do.'

Perry smiled, started the car, and drove back to the station.

At the end of the car park, he saw Susan Cunningham standing with her crutches, the lower half of one leg missing. Part of him felt badly for her, but he tried to not stare at her with pitying eyes. She came over to the car, hauled herself in, putting the crutches into the back.

'You can look if you want,' said Susan.

'Sorry,' said Perry. 'It's not easy.'

'I'm sure it isn't.'

'Well, you were always dynamic, Susan, and now—'

'Is this meant to be a pep talk that's going to help, Perry? If it's not, it's probably not worth saying it.'

'You'll get back up,' he said. 'Prosthetic. That's what you'll need. They have those runners, don't you? Sorry, nobody's going to make it any easier with their advice, are they?'

'You do,' said Susan. 'You're the first person who's spoke to me about it. Everybody else just stares. Do you know that?'

'You deserve better than that. Anyway, you think you're fit enough to go into this house?'

'Of course I am,' she said. 'What else could happen?'

'Well, I wouldn't make you come out, except—well—that's Macleod's rule, isn't it? This whole killer thing. Worried that some of us are going to get attacked. It's just an address for flowers, so I doubt there's going to be anything there. It's probably not even his address. He probably just picked them up from somebody. He probably stood outside.'

'We've got to check it,' said Susan. 'So, let's go.'

Perry drove across the city and past an industrial state to a quiet set of houses. The address was a single house on its own, detached but small. Perry approached the front door, looked in through frosted glass but could see no one. He walked round the back. Again, there was nobody about. It was just an average three-bedroom house from what Perry could make out. He rapped on the door and found it swung open.

'That's bizarre,' said Susan. 'Door open?'

'Let's take it easy,' said Perry. Perry went to step back, and then thought better of it, and walked into the house ahead of Susan. He stopped in the hall, scanning up and down, and said, 'Seoras is being very careful, isn't he?'

'It's a funny thing for Macleod to say. It gets in your head, I mean, we have to investigate. What's he expecting, some sort of trap? Some sort of—'

'Clarissa said that there were traps in the film. The police officers got caught in some. I guess that's why they're worried about them.'

'Well, they might not even use that part of the film, might they,' said Susan. 'It might just be the murders.'

'Best to be safe rather than sorry, though,' said Perry. He edged forward into the living room and looked across the sofa at the couple of magazines left out. Everything about the house said not lived in. There was no dirt, but there was a thin layer of dust. The place hadn't been used in a while.

'I don't think he's been in here,' said Perry. 'I'll maybe check upstairs. Do you want to try the kitchen out the back?'

'Of course,' said Susan. 'I'm just going to take a minute here.'

'What's wrong?' asked Perry.

'It's not sore,' she said. 'I've just had a moment.'

'What? With the leg?'

'The thing is, Perry, you keep feeling like it's still there. It's like the leg hasn't gone. You know, it's like . . .' Susan stopped for a moment. Perry came closer. She reached out with both arms and put her face onto his shoulder. He heard her weep.

'It's not there, Perry. It's gone. My leg's gone. I—it won't be the same,' she said.

'What do you mean?' said Perry. 'I mean, it's never going to be the same to walk on, is it? But you'll learn to walk again with—'

'No, not that,' said Susan. 'Who's going to want me? If you know you're going to get intimate with someone, are they going to be looking at you? At my leg. Are they going to look at it and think, why is that strap on? Why is that bit of metal there? Is that going to kill the mood? Or if I take it off, are they going to look and think, where's her leg? What's the hell's wrong with her, what—'

'Stop,' said Perry. He pulled her close again, holding her tight, hearing her snivel. He let her fall backwards slightly, so her face looked up at him.

'They're going to think how lucky they are,' said Perry. 'They're going to think Susan Cunningham is the most gorgeous woman they've ever seen. They're going to think you're a goddess.'

'Really,' said Susan. 'You really think that?'

'Well, yeah,' said Perry. 'Yeah.' Perry could see in her eyes she hadn't understood him. She thought he was being kind, not honest. It wasn't the moment to say anything more.

Susan gathered herself together, stepped back out of his arms, and leant back on her crutches.

'I'll go upstairs,' said Perry, 'see if there's anything up there. In the meantime, you can wander out to the kitchen when you're ready.'

Susan nodded. Perry saw she was watching him all the way up the stairs. But it wasn't from any longing. More from needing reassurance. Sometimes he wished he didn't read people so well.

There were two bedrooms and a bathroom upstairs, but none of them looked untoward. The beds hadn't been slept in, though, and that thin layer of dust was everywhere. So what? Did he own this place? Perry would have to check the records.

Deciding to make his way back down the stairs, Perry reached the top of the landing. He stopped, seeing Susan was still where he had left her. She was leaning on her sticks, gathering herself together. He could run down, he could put a supportive arm underneath her, but he thought better of it. He would just let her get on, let her find that strength.

Perry sat quietly at the top of the stairs. Susan didn't see him but hopped down the hallway towards the kitchen. Perry remained seated as he heard her opening and closing drawers. Then she came back into the hallway. He stood up.

'I've checked the kitchen. There doesn't seem to be anything, Perry. I think there's a pantry out there, though. I'll look at it. See if it goes anywhere.'

'Okay,' said Perry. 'I'll be down shortly.'

Susan hobbled away down the hallway again, and Perry slowly made his way down the stairs. He watched her go through the door to the kitchen. And then he stopped, hearing her trying a door.

There was an almighty swish, like some mechanism had gone off. Then there was a clatter and Perry heard Susan cry out, along with a thud like something had hit the ground hard.

'Susan!' shouted Perry. But there was no response. Perry took off down the hallway. 'Susan! Susan!' he cried. He tore open the door to see a prone Susan Cunningham lying on the floor across the kitchen from him.

Interlude 3

Of course, you know what the difference is between men and women, don't you? I know you're looking at me as if I've said something daft. But there is a distinction.

You turn up at a house and give a man some flowers, he'll look at you suspiciously. You turn up at a house and give a woman flowers, and they're looking for the good in you. They're looking for what is right about you. Flowers do things for women. I've never understood it, but I know how to work it.

Of course, you don't just turn up; you've got to lay down the groundwork. But you can do that; you'll be good at it. You'll learn from me how to do it. Sometimes you might have to do a little research. You might not understand the type of flowers that she likes, but whatever, make sure that you present those flowers not too long after you've met her.

She can't suspect anything; got to go along with it. She's got to be part of the plot; got to be completely trusting in you when you take her to her end. It's important, very important. And that's where flowers come in.

Flowers gain you trust. Flowers gain you an honesty that

you don't have. Trust me. Flowers. Flowers is where she'll fall down. Trust me.

Chapter 09

'Susan!' cried Perry, but Susan was holding a hand up. She was chest on to the ground with her face turned sideways. Her good leg was lying prone, and her short leg was on top. But a hand was held up to Perry.

'Don't move,' said Susan. 'I'm not convinced this is over.'

Perry looked down. Susan's crutches were damaged. The hollow tubes had been hacked in hard and one of them was almost broken off. They'd also been thrown away on the floor. As Perry looked down beyond Susan, he could see a large blade buried into the woodwork of the kitchen cupboards. It was round about the height a person's ankles would be.

'What on earth was that?' asked Perry, not moving.

'I came in, and all of a sudden, something swept the crutches away from me. Looks like it's damaged them.'

'It's damaged them all right. You're not going to be able to use those,' said Perry.

'I don't know if anything else is going to come. I'm not sure I can get up either. Not without—'

'Stuff the crutches,' said Perry. 'We need to get you up. We need to get you out of here in case anything else happens.'

'Don't move,' said Susan. 'You don't know if there's anything else. You don't.'

Perry picked up his mobile and put a call in to the station. 'I need Jona,' he said when he got through to the forensic lab.

'Miss Nakamura is busy.'

'I don't care,' said Perry. 'This is DC Warren Perry, and I need her now. It's potentially a matter of life and death.'

Jona got to the phone approximately thirty seconds later.

'Perry, Jona! Life and death—what are you on about?'

'I'm standing in the house of our supposed killer. On the floor is Susan. There was a blade that came out to take her ankles off. Fortunately, I think she was in mid-hop with her crutches. The blade took the crutches out, left her on the floor, and I'm standing close by. We're worried the place might have more booby traps. I would help her but I don't want to move.'

'Okay,' said Jona, 'I can't really advise from this distance. I'm on my way, Perry. Don't move. Okay? Don't move. If nothing is activated at the moment, don't move.'

Perry closed the call. He put his phone away in his pocket. He looked down at Susan Cunningham.

'She said, "Don't move."'

'And that's the advice. That's the expert advice. Don't move. I've only got half a leg on one side. And I've no crutches anymore. Don't move.' Susan laughed.

'What are we going to do?' asked Perry.

'We're going to not move,' said Susan. 'How are you?'

Perry was aware his hands were shaking.

'I'm okay,' he said.

'He said, gritting his teeth,' said Susan. 'It's the lack of the cigarettes, isn't it? It's getting to you now. This situation's getting to you. Without them.'

'I could really do with one,' said Perry. But he decided he

needed to overcome, rather than succumb to the cigarettes.

Whilst they were waiting, Perry decided to lighten the mood. 'Susan,' he said, 'do you think if I washed my clothes enough that the smell of the cigarettes would go away?'

'Probably,' she said. 'Why?'

'Because I can't tell. I've never been able, really, to smell my clothes with the cigarettes on them. So—'

'This really isn't helping you, is it?' she said. 'Are you trying to give them up?'

'I am giving them up,' said Perry. 'I'm not trying. I am. At the moment I just feel a bit cold turkey.'

'You are shaking but you're under high stress level. It doesn't matter if you have one.'

'Of course it matters. It always matters,' he blurted.

'You can always take those patches.'

'People always say that. There's something about it being in your hand, though. There's something about it being there that makes it work. Eases you.' Perry continued to stand as the silence filled the room. Susan looked up at him.

'Perry, you know something? You've been fantastic with this issue I've had. I don't forget that you were there, that you saved me.'

'Anybody would have done it for you.'

'Yes, but it was you,' said Susan. 'It was you that did it. If we get out of here, let's go for a drink sometime, not as detectives, but as friends.'

Perry could feel the blood pumping inside of him. *What was it she was asking of him? They needed to be colleagues. After all, she was working with him. Could he keep it there? Could they do that? Was it the right thing to do to be more social? Be more than social?*

'Well, we can go for a drink. Do something interesting.'

'Good,' she said. 'I don't think I'm going to get out of the office much for the rest of this case. Look at my sticks.'

'You can always get your new sticks, can't you?' said Perry.

'Yeah, but Macleod will hit the roof with this. You'll see, I won't be allowed out. I'll be declared unfit to do anything but office work. Especially now he's taken over.'

Perry commiserated with her but he saw the mess of her crutches and thought that maybe the office might be best.

Cars were heard pulling up outside the house. Susan gave a smile. 'I'll be out of here soon,' she said. Jona came into the building first.

'Don't move,' said Jona. She heard Macleod coming in behind her. 'And you keep out until I've said this is safe.'

Jona, dressed in her forensic outfit, had a small bag of tools with her. She got to the edge of the kitchen and she started tapping things.

'It's in here somewhere,' she said.

It took Jona about ten minutes to check everywhere thoroughly and make sure there were no more traps. She smiled at Cunningham and Perry, giving an all clear but told them not to linger and just get out. Perry bent down, sweeping an arm underneath Cunningham's good leg and one around her back. He carried her out to the front of the house, setting her down on a stone step.

'What on earth?' said Macleod.

'There was a blade,' said Susan. 'I was in the kitchen. I'd just put the sticks down and was swinging in when this blade came right underneath me. Took my sticks out. I think it was designed to take the ankles off.'

'I'm beginning to despise this guy,' said Macleod. 'He's

bugging me.'

'It's not surprising,' said Perry. 'That's what the film said, wasn't it? He's going to look to get in under your skin. And now you're in charge of the case, well.'

'What?' said Macleod.

'You won't thank me for saying this, Seoras, but now we've got a celebrity on the case. It'll garner more attention. Whether he's doing that for the film release coming up, or whether he's just doing it because he sees you as a grander target, I don't know.'

Jona arrived out of the house. 'You don't go in there until I have been through with my team and checked in case there's any more booby traps.'

'Of course,' said Macleod. 'And you don't go anywhere,' he said to Susan.

'Why?'

'Because you're missing a leg and you've just had your sticks taken off you. You could have lost your other foot in there.'

'Well, at least there was only one to go after,' said Susan. Macleod looked at her in horror, and then saw her laughing. 'Sorry, that was a close call. Got to try to keep it funny. If you don't, you fall apart,' said Susan.

Macleod shook his head. 'Perry, what have we got on the flowers, though?'

'We got here,' he said. 'I don't know what it's going to show us. I guess you're going to have to wait.'

Macleod picked up his mobile and placed a call to Ross. 'Ross, I know you're not out and about, but you need to be careful. We're encountering booby traps. I think we're being set up.' Ross thanked him, but Ross was still in the office. He called Clarissa.

'I'm just about to get on the plane to London, Seoras. Don't think we'll be in trouble. I mean, we're quite far away.'

'Nonetheless, have you got Patterson with you? You've got to be careful. Wherever you go into, you need to be careful. All right? Cunningham near lost her other foot.'

'Is she okay?'

'She'll live,' said Macleod. 'But I'm going to confine her to the office. You've got to be fleet of foot. You've got to be—'

'I get it, Seoras, okay? But I'm off to interview the arts people, doing the glamour bit. Don't worry about me. I'm an old dog. I've seen enough stuff.'

Macleod closed down the call and turned back to Perry and Susan.

'Let's see what we get from in here. What do you think?'

'I think the next killing is just around the corner,' said Perry.

'What do you mean?' asked Macleod.

'You've taken over the case. As soon as you have, you nearly had somebody end up in a serious accident. I think we've been doing well not to have succumbed.'

'You think he intended this?' asked Macleod.

'The trap, yes. This is the warning like in the film. Clarissa said the film had this in it. We have the police being attacked; we have several incidents. You've run it by the book and ended up here. But now we know what we're looking at, so there's going to be a different sort of booby trap. There's going to be other things in front of us,' said Perry. 'This is the start of it, Seoras. We need to be careful. Really careful.'

'You don't have any other cigarettes,' said Macleod.

'No,' said Perry. 'Why?'

'Because I feel like taking it up at the moment.' He turned and walked away, standing aloof from the rest of them.

'Is he okay, do you think?' asked Susan.

'He's thinking,' said Perry. 'And he's thinking hard, Susan. We could be in trouble with this one. Real trouble.'

Interlude 4

The perfect trap is one in which they never see it coming. And the thing about detectives that you'll come to understand is, when they find something, they're not wary of it.

It's the excitement; it's an adrenaline chase. It's like the world has just become perfect to them and they can't resist because this was hidden. And if it was hidden, somebody was stopping them from finding it. So, you have to hide something from them. Make them work to reveal it. And when they've revealed that and they feel they've earned it, they chase along.

They won't keep a clear head. It's like they stop thinking and they just charge. Charge on in and sort out whatever it is. And that's when you have them. When they're on the charge. When they're in that moment.

The perfect trap also doesn't appear in your face. Everybody's looking forward when they go somewhere. They're peering to see what's there. Very few look down. When you go into cities, people don't look up. They say, oh, what's this shop? Isn't that a smart lintel above that door? Isn't that a nice door? What's for sale?

Nobody looks up and says, look at the gargoyle features up

there. Look at the stonework. Nobody looks down into the sewers either. You want to make a trap; it comes from above or down below. It doesn't come from in front. The only other place to put it is behind, but that's harder to do.

The effective ones are the low ones or the high ones. You're not attuned to looking in that gap. It's like in baseball. When they pitch it, there's a certain zone. And the ball has to be in that zone, and they're swinging the bat. If it's not in that zone, they don't hit it. Because they're not expecting it to be there. It's a dud. It's no good. But in baseball, people still go for that dud. What we're doing is we're putting it out there in the wrong place. They react incorrectly because the ball's not where it should be and they get hit by it.

I'll teach you well but these things are a work of art. These things come from my mind and they work well. There isn't anything I've messed up with it. All you have to do is play your part. Get people in the right place.

The detective will be like the woman swayed by flowers, but with the allure of discovery. We let them solve things, place them where we want them. That's the key thing. And never ever show our face before them. Sometimes it's all about dangling the carrot, seeing if it'll take them off a cliff.

Chapter 10

'Just you mind your manners when this man arrives,' said Clarissa to Patterson. 'He must be in his, what, seventies at least, if not more. Might be deaf. Show some respect. These film people can be a bit funny sometimes.'

'I thought he was a cameraman,' said Patterson. 'He's not going to be eccentric, is he?'

'What do you mean by that?' asked Clarissa.

'Well, you find people at the top are much more eccentric. Dress a bit differently to everyone. Maybe don't follow the rules. Whereas somebody like a cameraman, he's going to be more staid, more . . . professional, more detached from it.'

Patterson became aware that Clarissa was staring at him. He hadn't intended it as a comment on his own team, but he could see that she was taking it that way.

'Like I say, just be respectful. Always respectful, especially of those people at the top.'

'I shall follow your pristine example,' said Patterson.

Clarissa sat back and sipped her coffee. He was certainly fitting into the team, Patterson, and giving her a bit more lip than he ever had done. It was a good thing, because he was more relaxed, and a relaxed Patterson worked well. But, she'd have to tow him in sometimes, make sure he didn't get out of hand. She was the boss, after all.

An older man approached the maître d'. He had grey hair, and was wearing a beige pair of slacks, with a beige jacket over it. Having given a name to the maitre d', the man followed the head waiter directly over towards Clarissa's table.

'Hello!' said Clarissa, standing up. 'Hello! Hello!' She indicated for Patterson to join her. 'You must be Ron Boland.'

'Ron Boland at your service, ma'am.'

'I'm Detective Inspector Clarissa Urquhart. This is Detective Constable Eric Patterson. Thank you for coming.'

'Well, thank you for bringing me here.'

'Would you like a coffee or something? Some of their pastries are quite good,' said Clarissa.

'Why, thank you,' said Ron. He had his seat pulled out for him, and sat down. Ron was given a menu by the maitre d'. After he'd taken a brief glance and ordered, Ron turned and looked at Clarissa.

'Clarissa, I have to say I'm a little surprised to be getting a call, especially about a film from so far back. I know it's going on tour, but really, I didn't think people would want to talk to someone like me.'

'I'm afraid I'm here in a professional capacity,' said Clarissa. 'You see, there's been a murder, and it's been carried out in a way that is extremely similar to the murder in the first part of *The Slaughterhouse*.'

'Well, it wasn't me,' said Ron. 'You can check. I've been here in London the whole time. I've been—'

'We're not here to accuse you of anything,' said Clarissa. 'I'm here to understand about the film, about the production, about what happened around it. I've got to be honest, Ron;

if anybody from the cast or crew carried out this murder, it would be quite impressive. You're one of the youngest surviving members.'

'Well, I was only in my very early twenties when we shot it,' said Ron. 'They couldn't really afford more experienced cameramen, and some of them wouldn't take it on given the content of the film. I was up and coming and, frankly, was quite excited by the role. So, yes, that's why I got it.'

'What was it like on set?' asked Clarissa. 'I know it's a long time ago, but if you could kind of bring it back.'

'There was a lot of friction,' said Ron. 'It was one of my first productions, not my absolute first, but one of my first. And like the ones I'd been on previously, there was always a fraught-ness about the filming. Some directors are chaotic. But you have to get things done. So there's a lot of sharpness, although there's a lot of angst at times. And we had a lot of friction.'

'And what was that caused by?' asked Patterson.

'You've got to understand, we were putting a film out at the time that was very different to the mainstream. There was a lot of gratuitous violence. There was quite a lot of nudity, graphic images, so that's why it got banned. But if you can imagine, filming some of this stuff wasn't pleasant. The killings and things that went on in it, they were done well, in the sense that there was realism to them.

'Given that, and the large amount of nudity and sexual deviance, it wasn't a normal film set. You had actors and actresses who were in positions that they weren't used to—various ages as well. Remember that our leading lady was only eighteen back then. There was a lot of friction about that. I think nowadays there would be a lot more said about it.'

'How did you find working on it then?' asked Clarissa. 'With all this going on?'

'It was kind of crazy for the crew. I'm used to being told, get your set-up done; we're filming at this point. And, yeah, that's the way most films worked. You worked hard as a crew, but you had timescales. We had lots and lots of meetings going on in this one, especially from the cast. The crew, not so much. As the crew, you just get paid. You take your money; you do your job.

'Not so with the cast because of the things they were being asked to do. There was constant rewriting, constant meetings. People not wanting to be a part of certain scenes. It was quite something.'

'Did you enjoy working on it?' asked Patterson.

'Well, it was exciting as well as being traumatic. You'll remember this was quite a big deal for me. The camera work was praised,' said Ron. 'I'm not one to blow my trumpet, but it was held up as being extremely good.'

'I watched it recently,' said Clarissa, 'and it's not an easy watch, but you are right. Your camera work was good. However, is there anything else about it that struck you?'

'Well, I've got to be honest. We were doing some amazing stuff with mechanisms. If you've seen the film, you'll know what I'm talking about. There are certain scenes with deaths that occur, and we had to build mechanisms for them. Of course, they're all made safe, but some of them you saw were truly terrifying.

'Some where people get punctured, one where somebody gets thrown into the air, coming off a roof, but that was done by propelling them. We also had to have camera tracks because of the angles that were being done. You had to be on a camera track and the camera would run. The build of it was amazing. It enabled us to keep the camera steady and yet do some of these dynamic motion shots.'

'I get you with that,' said Clarissa, 'but these mechanisms you talked about, you said they were amazing. In what way?'

'Well, they were amazing in many ways,' he said. 'Because, frankly, the ideas of some of them were pretty sick. But we carried them out and made them, the machine part of them. You couldn't buy any of this off the shelf. This was all made in a workshop.'

'And who made them?' asked Clarissa.

'Stephen Fritz. Or Fitzy, as we called him, God rest his soul. Absolute genius.'

'What was he like on the film set?'

'A quiet soul in some ways. Very good with people like ourselves. Technical people. I would talk about the camera runs and what I wanted built, and he understood. He could give me technical feedback and I could share that with him. He was excellent.'

'What was he like with the director?'

'Franz Kahn? What a guy that was. Absolute head bin,' said Ron. 'Hard work. He'd be pushing and pushing Stephen for these really top-notch machines which had to do this and that. They had to be safe at the same time while also making all the motions and to be quite frank, Stephen went and rebuilt stuff in time frames that were just crazy. All because Franz wanted to change the shots slightly, wanted to put something in a different position.

'I think that's what got to Stephen and that he got no credit because nobody says and thinks about the machinery. Well, in some ways they do. You take in the camera work, because you're seeing it, but everything else is just a thing. You think about the acting. He kind of got left out.'

'But you said he died a few months ago.'

'I think so,' said Ron. 'As far as I'm aware, he died. I remember there was an invitation to the funeral, or maybe just a mention of it. He didn't have any family either. I didn't get to it, though.'

'And what about Franz Kahn? He's still alive, isn't he?' asked Clarissa.

'Yes. Ninety, now. There's him; there's me. There's the grip, O'Donnell, I think, because he was very young. And then there was our starlet, Sophie. Everybody loved Sophie. Some of them tried to *love* Sophie, if you get my meaning, but she was quite innocent in some ways.

'I think she was pretty shocked by what the film involved. Maybe traumatised. Yeah, I think that's fair. It's funny, isn't it? Because as a film, it's taken cult status because of what it was at the time. Nowadays, do they make things anywhere near as shocking? Of course they do. Some of it's more shocking, I think. But, at the heart and soul of it all, were the people who were working on it. It affected them; it affected us, me.'

'Overall, though,' said Clarissa, '—and think about all aspects of the film—is there anybody who was on that set you would think might have had such a problem that they'd want to highlight it in a graphic way, i.e., by a very public murder?'

'No,' said Ron, 'why wait till now? I mean, even if I wanted to, I couldn't think how to do it, you know? I'm too old for that. Too old to run around trying to sort out what you'd have to do. I mean, you tell me what you'd have to do. You said it was a killing.

'If it was that first one in the film, well, you'd have to be pretty strong, wouldn't you? You'd have to be able to pick up whatever poor woman you'd killed off and dump her down from the top of a cinema. I don't think I could pick up someone like that these days. Picking up a cup of coffee is enough. It's very good, by the way. Very good. This bun. Wow! Delicious.'

Clarissa kept the conversation going, but really, she'd learned enough. She'd go to Sophie. If she'd been traumatised, maybe she'd have a reason for carrying out murders. Although Clarissa didn't see it quite that way. But she might have more gossip.

Fitz sounded good, but he was dead. There was the grip, as well. And there was Khan. Certainly, Ron Boland didn't seem to be a man who was capable of murder. Certainly not such energetic murder.

After Ron Boland departed, Clarissa sat with her coffee, tapping away on the side of the mug with her nails. She looked up to see it was annoying Patterson, so she continued to do it.

'Look,' said Patterson, 'we're barking up the wrong alley with this. Could just be a copycat.'

'Of course, we could be barking up the wrong alley,' said Clarissa; 'we could be completely off the track here. Macleod wants to know all about the film, he wants to know about the people in it. Sometimes, well, something as dramatic as filming this, it can set things off in people, and it can come back later in life.'

'Yes, but Boland makes a good point. You need to be pretty fit to carry out a lot of these killings.'

'If you carried them out yourself! There's that recent case that Hope had, contract killing. They could hire somebody to do this, specify how it should happen.'

'Well, I suppose that's a point,' said Patterson. 'What's our next move, then?'

'I think we're off to find our actress. Let's see what she says about it all.'

Just as she was about to leave the rather posh restaurant, Clarissa's phone vibrated. She picked it up.

'This is Jona.'

'Hiya,' said Clarissa. 'What can I do for you?'

'I take it you heard about the incident with Susan?'

'Yeah, some sort of booby trap or that. I've been talking to the cameraman on the original film. The guy that made all those traps is dead.'

'I just wanted to mention,' said Jona, 'that the device that sought to take off the feet of Susan Cunningham was very well made. It's a great bit of craftsmanship. The devices in the film, and I'm asking you because I know you've seen it, they're quite wicked, aren't they?'

'Very.'

'Well, follow down those lines. See if you can find anybody who can build them, and where they would build them as well.'

'Like I said, the man who made them all originally is dead. Stephen Fitz.'

'Well, we all have prodigies,' said Jona. 'Just keep an eye out for them, okay?'

'Of course,' said Clarissa. 'Anyway, I have to go. I'm off to meet a beautiful actress.'

'All the stars talk to you!'

'Yours talk to you too, don't they?'

'Not with their mouths, though,' said Jona. 'They're usually dead.'

'Well, I'm going to see someone who may have been traumatised by the film. But I'll bear the machines in mind. See if she knows anything more.'

'Very good,' said Jona, 'Let me know if you find anything.'

Clarissa closed the call and, together with Patterson, they walked to the little green sports car. It would be a reasonable journey to find the actress. A quick check on her phone said she was heading for Wales. Clarissa just hoped she'd be at home.

Interlude 5

The shock of surprise. Most people think that being surprised is a nice thing. Some people don't get that surprise is not a good thing. Especially when you're truly not ready for it. You're truly not waiting.

If somebody can get you thinking on a different plane, and then suddenly in comes crashing this surprise, it can easily destroy you. We're quite sensitive creatures at heart. We struggle with the turmoil of change, but fast, undeniable, difficult-to-get hold of change—that's the stuff that really messes you about.

The other thing about surprise is you cannot see it coming. No true surprise. True surprise starts a shock that drives at your core. It's surprise makes you rock. You cannot see that coming. Everything must look normal and then suddenly, bam, it interferes with your head because you can't see the process.

You can't see the process, and if you can't see reason, be it moral, be it physical, be it any other reason, if you can't see that, it's really going to mess you up. This will mess them up. It will mess up anybody that sees it, I think.

Chapter 11

John and Debbie's relationship was never easy. John thought it would have been smoother now that they were both eighteen. But their overbearing parents were still keen on controlling what they did. His mother was watching him like a hawk, pestering his father. They were worried because his older brother David had got a girl into trouble, as his father had put it, and John wouldn't be doing the same. John had no intentions of getting into trouble. Rather, he understood the practices of safe sex, and so did Debbie. They didn't want a kid.

Debbie and John had been seeing each other for nearly three months and Debbie's parents watched John like a hawk, too. They were well aware of what his brother had done, of the mini scandal it had caused. Debbie would not end up that way. Debbie complained to John constantly, saying about how her mother was asking where she was going, who she was with. It was almost like needing a chaperone.

Debbie had read, unlike John, many of the Regency novels. In those tales, young women were always escorted, always chaperoned, until they were married off. Debbie felt like they were in a Regency drama, but she had faith in John and their relationship. The two of them were constantly conspiring to get away.

They had found their place to go, although it wasn't a salubrious one. There was an alleyway in town, a bit of a side path that nobody seemed to use. And down it, jutting into one side, was a little alcove. Above the alcove was a concrete roof. It didn't reach into the alleyway, but it did at least mean that the rain was kept off them. They'd been there several times now, always watching, making sure that nobody was following them. But once there, they could be alone.

It was somewhere to be alone. They weren't getting themselves into trouble, as his mother would have put it, and they weren't flinging clothes here, there and everywhere. It was somewhere to sit, cuddle, talk, and be intimate in all the other ways that didn't involve a bed.

John found it funny that his parents always seemed to think the worst of him, just because of his brother. Didn't they understand people could be practical about these things, even though they were still teenagers?

Today had been a case in point and they were thankful to one of Debbie's friends, although, in fairness, it was cutting both ways. Debbie's friend Joanne was keen to get away with her own boyfriend and had told her mother that she was with Debbie. Debbie had told her parents she was with Joanne.

John hadn't been mentioned, and neither had the other boyfriend and, for some bizarre reason, this was waylaying suspicion. Of course, as long as nobody phoned looking for anyone. But they were eighteen now. The days of phoning were different. They didn't call each other's parents; they called you on your mobile and if Debbie was in the alleyway with John, she had ways and means of answering so that they didn't hear John. Either that or she let it ring out and texted them immediately, saying she was in the middle of watching a film. Anything to waylay them.

So today, Debbie and Joanne had met up with the boys and then gone their separate ways. John had taken Debbie down to a fast-food joint in town. They'd sat over diet cokes and fried chicken before taking a stroll down by the river in Inverness. From there, they walked out of the town centre to the residential areas before they spotted their alleyway.

As they got close, Debbie looked up at a nearby roof and saw a man working. He was up fixing what looked like an old TV aerial. She didn't know if it truly was one. Everything was on the internet these days, but the man was working on something. John had glanced up at him and taken no notice. Debbie asked if the man could see into the alleyway.

'No,' said John. 'He's still quite a distance from it. He'd have to spring, oh, a good ten feet. Ten feet across and then peer down and in before he could look down the alleyway. And even then, we'll be in the alcove. Nobody's seen us every time we've gone. We've been up this way for months now,' he said to Debbie. 'You really shouldn't be worried. This is perfect.

'Come on,' said John, taking Debbie's hand and dragging her along. She was wearing a large raincoat, but the hood was down, and her blonde hair was rolling down onto her back. John liked it when she untied it, although Debbie said it was quite a fuss to keep it that way.

His father had said she was one of the plainer girls, but that's what John liked about her. She didn't fuss with the make-up. She didn't have eyebrows that looked like they were painted on, with eyelashes that looked like they were garden rakes. And when she smiled, the world was just made up for John.

Together they entered the alley before Debbie suddenly stopped, looking up. 'Are you sure he can't see down here?' she said.

How, after all this time, thought John, *could she get so nervous?* They'd been here before and yes, there'd been nobody up on the roof, but there'd been others walking about in the street. Others that had bothered her. She was worried about her parents, frightened if they found out that she had gone behind their back, she would be grounded and taken away from John. It was funny how those Regency novels seemed so modern day in some ways.

'There is no way he can see down,' said John in a hushed whisper. 'Come on, get to the alcove. You'll feel better in there. You always do.'

'I suppose so,' she said, still peering up at the roof.

John turned and looked up with her. The alleyway was cut in between two sections of terrace. It ran through to a street at the back, and the alcove was maybe some twenty feet in. On the other side was steep red brick until you got to the alcove.

John always thought it was a funny building. He stared up at the roof.

'Look Debbie, if he was on his front, lying up there and actually looking down, he still couldn't see into the alcove. We'll go into the corner, tuck in tight, if that helps.'

'Sorry,' she said, 'I'm just—you know I get nervous now. You know how Mum and Dad have been. Your brother really screwed it up for everybody.'

'You don't have to tell me that,' said John. 'Oh, come on,' he said, taking her hand. He tugged it gently, and she turned and smiled at him.

'You're good with me; do you know that?' she said. 'You

never push me.'

'You're just being daft,' he said. His tone was affectionate, and he pulled at her arm gently. She relented, walking behind him up the alley until they reached the alcove.

There'd been rain earlier on in the day and the alleyway still had signs of wetness on the ground, but inside the alcove, it was all dry. The predominating wind of the city meant that the alcove would have had the rain at its back and, with the concrete roof, it never got wet. It was one of the things that John liked about it.

He sat down inside the alcove and made a space for Debbie to sit in front of him. He wrapped his arms around her belly, pulling her in tight and resting his chin on her shoulder.

'We're here now,' he said. 'It's our safe place. It's a place where we can be us.'

'Are you sure he can't see?' said Debbie. 'My feet might stick out.'

John let go a sigh. The irritation in him was clear, but he was trying to be gentle. She was being paranoid, after all.

'He can't see,' said John. 'Look!' He stood up and gave Debbie his hand and lifted her up as well. Together they leaned out, peering at the corner, up towards the roof.

'What can you see of that roof?' said John. 'How much can you really see?'

'I know what you're saying but if he came down.'

'If he comes down any farther, he'd fall off and land in the alleyway,' said John. 'That's not going to happen. These people aren't daft. Besides, if you're up there working on the roof, the last thing you're going to be doing is paying any attention to what's going on below. You've got to watch your footing up there. People that do this, they're very focused. They're not bothered about anything below. They're bothered about what's around them.'

'I guess you're right,' said Debbie. 'I don't know. That's probably how it's going to work, isn't it? Sorry.'

She turned and kissed him. John wrapped his arms around her, and they spent a moment before John beckoned Debbie to sit down again. Once more, he lowered himself to the ground, near a space in front of him, and then wrapped his arms around her. His chin sat on her shoulder, and he felt her head leaning in towards his. And there they sat until two minutes later when Debbie said, 'Maybe he can see us.'

'No, he can't,' said John. Now he was getting agitated. 'He really can't. Look, Debbie, I'm not being funny, but you're letting this go to your head. I mean, you're not being sensible about this at all, are you? And anyway, if he saw us, what's he going to do? How on earth is he going to get back to your folks?'

'Paranoid? Things always get back to my folks,' she said, 'always. I thought you would have realised that by now. It's like they have this ability; they can pull rumour in from anywhere, a random observation. The other week, I got questioned for over an hour because I was ten minutes late coming out of the swimming pool.'

'What did they question you for?'

'Because you were seen around the area, but I was only in talking to Joanne, just gassing, talking away about stuff. I didn't even see you.'

'No, I didn't see you,' said John. 'Seriously, they were on at you.'

'On and on and on over dinner. They've got nothing else to do except talk about me. You wouldn't believe it John. It's so boring; it's so completely and utterly boring and all you get is the n'th degree. Following that, my mum went and checked out my swimsuit.'

'Your swimsuit?'

'Yes. She had the idea that I would go in my bikini and not my swimsuit. I was going to swim, so I took my swimsuit, you know, the same as when I'm training,' she said. 'But she had the idea that I would have packed my bikini. I haven't worn it since two summers ago. I'm not sure it even fits,' said Debbie.

'That's rough,' said John. But his mind was elsewhere, wondering about that bikini, though he didn't show it. Instead, he held her tight and said to her, 'Nobody sees us here. Nobody's ever talked about the alcove. This is our place. Nobody can interrupt it. Nobody can find us. We'd hear them if they ever came into the alleyway. We've had nobody walk through in all that time. No one. There are no windows down the side here.'

'I know,' said Debbie, 'and it's great. It really, really is. I'm just—I've got a bad feeling today. A terrible feeling.'

'Let me take the feeling away then,' said John. He moved his arms from around her belly and began to rub her shoulders. She leaned back.

'That's better,' she said. 'How do you do that? How did you get good at it? I mean, you haven't been trained to do it.'

'I'm just made for you,' said John.

'That's so cheesy,' laughed Debbie.

But it had the effect John wanted. Debbie needed to chill out. She needed to relax. She needed to enjoy this time when they were together.

'There's no way he can see, is there? No way?'

'The only way he's going to see is if he comes off that roof and plonks himself right down here in front of this alcove. And what's the likelihood of that?' asked John.

An explosion rocked the air. It wasn't one of those catastrophic ones, where you get to your feet and run for your life, fearing that buildings would topple. It wasn't surreal like that. More like a loud bang you would hear on stage. The one that would make you jump in the theatre. The one that would make you turn and stare in the street.

'What the—?' cried John. He could feel Debbie suddenly tense up. He was tense, too. *Where did it come from? What was it?* He was about to get up to his feet when there was a sudden thud right in front of him. It was caused by something dropping quickly onto the ground. It was something, however. A large something.

There was a loud crack of bones, a grunt, and then in front of him, lying completely still, was the man from the roof. His head had caved in, and blood was running out, Debbie screamed, but John stood looking in disbelief.

'How?' shouted Debbie. 'How?'

John said nothing, but simply stared.

'We've got to get out of here. We need to go!' shouted Debbie,

'No,' said John. 'Look at him; we've got to tell somebody; we've got to—,'

'But my parents,' said Debbie,

'Stuff your parents. That guy needs help,' said John. But as he stared at him, he wasn't sure if any help was going to be good enough for the man who had fallen from the sky.

Chapter 12

Hope McGrath drove her car through Inverness, parking up just inside the police cordon. It had segregated off the alleyway where the latest body had been deposited. There was a bustle of activity from the local uniform police, and she could also see Susan Cunningham hopping about on her crutches. Hope found the woman remarkable, but wondered would there be a payback to come?

She had brought Susan in after the incident when her leg had been amputated. Returning to work, Hope had followed the procedures to make sure that Susan was okay and fit for duty. Susan had wanted to come back. She told Hope that sitting at home would just be hell for her.

Hope wondered what sort of life she had outside of work. Well, given her recent past, maybe she put her time in by dating too many people. It wasn't something Hope was going to push. But she looked at her constable, amazed at her, but also wondering just how fragile she was underneath. Macleod had told her to remain at a desk, but this was a crime scene, not an unknown to be investigated.

Hope marched forward, intercepting Susan on her travels.

'How are we doing?'

'It's all sealed off. I'm trying to get Jona sorted at the moment. She's been up top.'

'Up top,' said Hope. 'That's just the roof, isn't it? Do we think somebody was up there? I take it we've sealed it.'

'It's not been a person,' said Susan. 'It's a device.'

Hope looked at her. 'A what?'

'A device. Our victim was launched off the roof by an exploding panel. Like a trap. It fired up, launching him into the air. Now it didn't catapult him that far, but far enough to take him off the roof, to fall into the alley.'

'You serious?' asked Hope.

'It happens in the film. Apparently somebody was fired off a roof.'

'I read what Clarissa said about the murders, about them dying, but I didn't think they'd actually be able to do it like this.'

'What?' said Susan. 'Set a trap? Everything seems to be the setting of traps. Or something of that ilk. Apparently, there's lots of them in the film. I'm still struggling to get time to watch it. It's been hectic since everything started.'

'Are we okay to look at it?'

'If we get suited. As I say, Jona's on scene. She's working from two places, massively far apart. The alleyway had a couple in it, and the guy basically crashed down right in front of them.'

'That was a bit of luck then,' said Hope, 'that they found this couple.'

'No,' said Susan, 'it wasn't luck. In the film, this man crashes down in the alleyway in front of a couple. It's played out.'

Hope stood in disbelief. 'That's quite something to take on

board,' she said. 'I want to get up and have a look at it.'

The two of them walked over to the forensic van, and picked up a couple of coverall suits. Hope was amazed at the lack of fuss Susan made about putting one on, despite having to wield her crutches two at a time in a single hand while doing it.

'Are you okay?' asked Hope. 'I mean—'

'I'm coping,' said Susan. 'You need me at the moment. We need to get on to this. I'm coping. I've lost a bit of my leg.'

'You have,' said Hope. 'And that would seem to me to be quite traumatic.'

'No, traumatic is Perry trying to give up cigarettes?' laughed Susan.

Hope wondered if she was masking, being brave despite feeling the loss underneath. Sure, the team had to put to the back of their mind problems and difficulties, but she'd lost part of her leg. This wasn't just something bad she'd seen in her head. The woman had physically lost her leg. She was going to have to think about options and get on through life without it. She'd need counselling; she'd need help; she'd need . . .

'Are we going?' asked Susan. 'I'm all right.'

Hope was aware that she'd suddenly been staring down at the missing leg. 'Sorry,' said Hope. 'It's just—'

'It's just what?'

'Nothing,' said Hope. 'You're right; let's get busy.'

Together they took the stairs inside of the house, eventually coming up towards the roof. There was access into the void of the roof from a room underneath and once up there, Hope could see the mechanism that had propelled the man off the roof. It was now lying open, where the roof panel would have been.

'Where did the panels go?'

'Crashed down. Much closer to the launch point.'

'How do you get this up here?' asked Hope. 'How do you actually physically build this? Build it with no one seeing.'

'Your difficulty is actually getting the parts into the building. Building it up here, provided you haven't got a large amount of noisy welding, cutting or that, is not a problem. If you cut off site, do that side of it elsewhere, as far as I can see, there's nothing that couldn't be brought in, in a reasonably sized bag. Sure, some of it might be heavy, but there's no part that looks to me like it would be obvious bringing it from a van or a car or that. You could hide most of it in bags.'

'Even so,' said Hope, 'how does nobody spot someone coming in with this?'

'I've taken a recce down through the building. The people that live here thought this was vacant up the top. They said there was a workman coming in over the last lot of months. They thought they were just getting it ready to rent it out.'

'Who does own it?' asked Hope.

'Cash payment. Council tax wasn't being paid, in fact isn't registered for that flat.'

'What?' asked Hope.

'Cash payment. The previous owner, now deceased—not under suspicious circumstances—took a cash payment. Spoke to his son on the phone. I think he was trying to bypass the inheritance tax. Son's been very forthcoming, now we've talked about a murder and saying we're not the ones going after him for some sort of tax avoidance or evasion.'

'Did he say who bought it off him?'

'It was a company. The man that turned up was quite indistinct. The description that's been given, it could be anyone, Hope. Older man, though.'

'So, we've got a dead body. A dead body in an alleyway caused by a machine that was built with no one's knowledge and an old man who nobody can really describe paying for the flat.'

'Exactly,' said Susan. She stood balancing on her crutches before lifting one up and pointing at the device. 'I think that's going to be key.'

'Where's Perry?' asked Hope.

'He was interviewing the two youngsters the man crashed down in front of. You want to speak to him?'

'I do. Come on. We'll go together. We need to put our heads together, work out what happens now, how we approach this.'

Susan was incredibly adept at getting up and down the stairs in the building. Hope had always known her as a fit woman, but she seemed to embrace the challenge of not having part of her leg. Was it possible that someone did just deal with it? Was it possible it was going to be simply a background event?

It would hit her at some other point. Hope knew that people grieved for loss of limbs, and she wondered if Susan was just delaying that process. Either way, she seemed very capable of operating as a constable. Hope needed all the help she could get.

As they left the building and turned towards the alleyway, Hope's phone rang and she picked it up.

'It's Seoras. I've just received another letter, and it's gone to the press. It's talking about the alleyway killing.'

'Does it say much else?'

'It's taunting us, well actually, it's taunting me by name.'

'Any clues in that, though?'

'Follows the line of the film. I checked with Clarissa. It's crazy,' said Macleod. 'They're following it exactly.'

'Can we get ahead of them, then? Can we get on top of it before the next one happens? I mean, what's the next killing?'

'A circus act,' said Macleod. 'The problem is they don't go to the same locations because it's all happening in a different place. This one could have been any roof in the town. There's no way we could have predicted this alleyway.'

'But there were two people watching him land. That's an incredible amount of observation,' said Hope. 'To find a place, to have a man working on the roof, then to have the victim crash down in front of a couple. That requires some planning. The film was the same, wasn't it?'

'Apparently so,' said Macleod.

'I'm going to speak to Perry. I need to find some more detail about these two youngsters,' said Hope. 'I'll speak to you soon.'

Hope put the phone away and marched over to the alleyway. As she did so, she saw Perry arriving.

'What have you got for me?' she asked.

'Well, I spoke to them—the two young ones. They've been coming here for quite a while. They said it's quiet; it's out of the way. There's a little alcove down this alley. They said nobody ever comes into the alley. Nobody has seen them. They've been, well, it's their spot. It's just where they go.'

'It's exposed for that sort of thing,' said Hope.

'They've not been doing that sort of thing,' said Perry. 'They've just been cuddling, holding each other, being with each other. It's not a—whatever that you're thinking of.'

Hope nearly rolled her eyes. A naïve assumption to make.

'They say that they heard the minor explosion and then he just landed right in front of them. The girl's totally traumatised,' said Perry. 'Absolutely traumatised.'

'And the boy?'

'He's in shock, too. John and Debbie. I've let the parents know. They weren't the best either. I mean, poor kids.'

'Do we think somebody's been watching them then?'

'Well, think about it,' said Perry. 'It's got to have been that well planned, hasn't it? To follow the film, they've got to make a man leap off a roof and land in front of the kids. And not just leap off. Actually, be physically sent by some sort of exploding device. Some sort of platform, lifting him off the roof, pushing him toward the alley.'

'So, the victim's got to be up there,' said Hope. 'The kids have got to be here in the alleyway. It's all timed together. How does he know where the kids are?'

'Must have followed them. Somebody was tailing them, and knows what they've been doing. Somebody's been watching them.'

'So, we see if anyone's contacted them.'

'Talked to the kids. They've been keeping this quiet from their parents. I talked to the parents. The parents had no idea they were here. Whoever's done this has been very good. It's been planned for a long time. They've built that device up there. Then they've said something's wrong with the TV aerial. The person's come up onto the roof from the side. They haven't gone up to the roof through the building.'

Hope looked around. There was still a mess in the alleyway. The body was covered by a tarpaulin, but the forensics team was still working. She could see the blood splatter. They were joined by Susan Cunningham.

'How do we go about this, Perry?' she asked. 'What do we do? What do you think, Susan?'

Perry gave Susan a moment to answer before he took up the

question.

'Devices,' he said. 'We need to go for the devices. They created a large swishing knife that nearly took off Susan's other foot. We also have now launched a person from up there. There's also the idea of hanging someone down from the roof of the cinema. You've got to have a bit of technical know-how with that, haven't you? You've got to know that you can drop them down a rope and it's going to be strong enough. There's someone here that's an expert.'

'Well, the expert on the film, according to Clarissa, is dead.'

'So, we've got somebody who worships his art then,' said Perry. 'I think we need to go on the line of attack of checking these machines.'

'Get Jona on to it, then. Jona, that's our technical person. Where is she?'

'That way,' said Susan. She went to hop off on her crutches, but Hope put her hand out. 'It's okay, I'll get her.'

Perry put his hand on Hope's shoulder and whispered quietly, 'Don't.'

'Actually, no; you get her. You get her, Susan,' said Hope. Cunningham hopped away on the crutches. Hope turned back to Perry.

'Let her do,' said Perry. 'She's struggling underneath, obviously. She needs help, but she's occupying herself at the moment. She's very good on the crutches, and that's a comfort to her, I think. Okay?'

'She will descend from this though, won't she? Susan will crash at some point. She will—'

'Grieve,' said Perry. 'Yes, I think so. But let her get on.'

A car pulled up on the edge of the cordon to be waved straight through, and Hope recognised who it would be. She saw Macleod get out of the car, his long coat blowing in the light breeze as he came closer.

'How's it going?' he asked. 'Was nearby when I called and couldn't keep away despite the call. What's happening?'

'Look at this,' said Hope. 'It's crazy. Somebody's built a device on that roof to launch somebody off it to land here. They've also timed the victim to land in front of a couple in their hideaway. They've followed the couple, keeping tabs on them, to arrange it so that someone's on the roof at the same time as they come here.'

'So they've been listening to them? They must have been able to check when they were coming out.'

'It's just nuts to build it up there, to—'

'More than one person,' said Macleod.

'Exactly what I was thinking,' said Perry.

'We need to be aware then,' said Macleod. 'I was thinking about the next murder. Circus setting. We've got circuses coming to Inverness soon. They're a few weeks off yet.'

'There's no idea of timescale though,' said Perry, 'is there? I mean, from the film.'

'No,' said Macleod. 'If you look at the timings in the film, it's not working in sync with these killings. The detail about each killing seems to be the same, certainly from what I can see in this one.'

'So, we may have time,' said Hope. 'We thought we should run the line of discovering how the machines are made and produced. I've asked Jona to come over.'

As if on cue, Hope heard the tap of Cunningham's crutches and saw Jona following her.

'How are we doing?' Macleod asked her and realised that he really should have left that for Hope to do.

'Up to my eyes,' said Jona. 'Crime scenes here, crime scenes there. We're trying to do two aspects to this as well. I'll see what I can do. See if we can pick up any DNA, but obviously we didn't get any matches from the last place. Trouble is, if they're not on the criminal record, we won't have them.'

'This is fresh, I suspect,' said Perry. 'This is a first time through. I haven't seen machines like this being used before.'

'Should we trace the machines?' asked Hope of Jona.

'Excellent line to go on,' said Jona, 'but I haven't got anyone. You'll have to bring someone in, an expert. I haven't got time to sit with him. I'm full to my gills, Seoras. Absolutely full.'

Macleod looked over at Susan. 'What about you?' he said. 'You think you could follow this, Susan? Get your teeth into it.'

'I don't have the mechanical expertise,' she said, 'but if you want me to.'

'Perry can handle these things. I've got Ross available too. Why don't you follow that line of attack? It would be a much better idea than having you race around here. Where is Ross, anyway?'

'He's pulling the CCTV, getting on top of that,' said Hope.

'Okay,' replied Macleod. 'Susan. Find us an expert. Get on to this.'

The team nodded and broke away, but Macleod told Hope to wait. He drew her across to a quiet corner.

'Look, I don't want to tell you how to run your job—'

'It's your job now though, isn't it?' said Hope. 'They pushed me to one side and brought you in.'

'Yes, they have. And it's my case. Don't get uppity on me, Hope. I need you for this. But I need you to take charge of Ross.'

'He's doing the CCTV because he's good at it.'

'We have got plenty of great people who can do the CCTV. They come from Uniform. He's used them before. Get Ross into the middle of this.'

'Is that an order?'

'No, it's not,' said Macleod. 'Look, I know you're peeved. I didn't agree with them bringing me in. That was their decision. It's an order. I can't walk away from that. So, I've split the investigation. I've kept Clarissa out of your hair for good reason. I need you doing what you're good at. And we need Ross being a DS. He's not the glamourous coffee boy anymore.'

Chapter 13

Macleod fought to stop himself from storming off the stage. The questions had been ridiculous. The press always wanted to blow things up. There was an air of high drama amongst them. They were almost painting an image of a comical guy. Either that or a genius, but someone two steps ahead of Macleod.

What annoyed Macleod was the guy was at least two steps ahead. If indeed, it was a guy. He needed to get ahead of him. He needed to anticipate what was happening. *No,* thought Macleod. *We need to find out who it is.*

As he stepped off the stage, he saw Susan Cunningham waiting in the wings. After making sure the press had dispersed, he took her to one side.

'What have you got?'

'I got a lecturer at the local technical college. David. David Bairstow. He's an engineering type of guy. Seems to put a lot of stuff together, anyway. Having talked to people up there, they said he's got an interest in a lot of the old movie sets and equipment. He could be very good. Certainly seems to know his stuff.'

'Oh, he's at the local technical college?' said Macleod,

brightly.

'Yes,' said Susan. 'I'm going to see him shortly.'

'No, you're not,' said Macleod. 'I'm coming with you. We're going to see him now.'

'He said he was just finishing something off.'

'This takes priority. We need to rope him in properly. He may not get a lot of his lecturing done over the next while. I want you to be working very closely with him. But just so he understands the importance, I'm coming for this first meeting with him. Don't let me undercut you. This is your game, your role. I'll drive you up though. How are you getting about otherwise?'

'Getting the uniform to drive me, or Perry if he's about.'

'I'll get a uniform to be assigned to you. Someone to be at your transport beck and call. I'll pay for it on the budget.'

'I can manage,' said Susan.

'No, you can't. I don't want you sitting wondering how you are going to get here, there, or wherever. You need to go where you want to go, when you want to go,' said Macleod. 'Stop being a martyr with this. You've got a problem and you're dealing with it. But don't act as if nothing's happened. We'll help you sort it, okay? So just take the help.'

He turned to walk off. Then he stopped. 'Sorry,' he blurted. 'That was just really, really badly put.'

'It was,' said Susan. 'But you're under pressure. Hope said that you never really enjoyed dealing with the press.'

'Did she now?' said Macleod. 'What else has she been saying about me?'

'She once told me you were the best there was.'

'Don't ever soft soap me,' said Macleod.

'Well, she said once you got past your grumpy exterior, you

were the best there was,' said Susan.

Macleod stared at the woman, trying to read her face, before he gave a grin. 'I can be grumpy,' he said. 'Usually because of other people. I appreciate you wanting to help. I appreciate you coming in. But if you say you're fit, I will treat you exactly the same as anyone else, except for the fact that you can't drive. So I'm going to make it so that you can get anywhere you want, when you want.'

'Yes, Inspector,' said Susan. It wasn't said harshly. She had a smile on her face and was letting him know she was going to follow his rank on this issue.

'In the meantime, I'm taking you up in the car,' said Macleod. 'Meet me down in the car park in five minutes.' As she went to walk away, he paused. 'How did you get new crutches so quick?' he said.

'I told someone I needed them,' she said. 'The other ones were mashed.'

'Are you okay after that?' he asked quickly.

'I'm running on not quite empty, but I'm running. It's like a car, isn't it? At the moment, it's going, so what we don't want to do is stop, because if we stop, starting it up again might not be that easy. You need me now, boss,' said Susan. 'Hope needs me, so we'll make do. But there's a time coming, and I'll need you.'

Macleod gave a small smile to her. 'Good,' he said. 'Good. That makes sense to me.'

It was approximately five minutes later when Macleod found Susan Cunningham standing beside his car. They drove up to the local technical college, where he pulled in and made straight for the front desk.

'Detective Chief Inspector Seoras Macleod,' he said to the

woman at the reception desk. 'I need to talk to David Bairstow. I don't care if he's in a lecture, nor do I care if he's in his office saying he can't be disturbed. I'm in the middle of a murder investigation and I need to speak to him. So, I'd be much obliged if he'd speak to me now.'

It wasn't rude, but it was certainly formal and to the point. Macleod sat down, and two minutes later, a small man, who was quite stocky, probably in his forties, and with black hair, approached Macleod. He wore grey trousers and a shirt with some stains on it. As he went to shake his hand, Macleod saw that his hand was not completely clean, like those who work with wood or in factories on the machines. There was always some sort of an oily sheen to them.

'David Bairstow. You must be the Detective Chief Inspector. I was just having to deal with the students, so I couldn't come straight away.'

'It's been two minutes,' said Macleod. 'I think that's fair. A very fast response. I apologise for pulling you away from your work, but I need you.'

'Okay,' said David. 'If you follow me up, we can speak in my office.'

Susan Cunningham sat beside Macleod on the opposite side of a desk from David Bairstow. They briefed the man on what was happening, and he looked thoughtful to Macleod.

'What would it take to have some of these devices built?' asked Macleod.

'From what you're describing, a lot of this stuff isn't something you'll just . . . how do I put this? You will get parts,' said David, 'but with custom builds, you might have to adjust them. You might have to build certain parts yourself. So, you're talking about someone who's used to dealing with precision engineering.'

'A lot of these devices were built initially in the film back in the sixties. Obviously, things have changed,' said Susan.

'Changed to a point with some of the machinery we've got, but it doesn't get any easier,' said David. 'You need to know what you're about. I can look at where you can buy such parts. You're also, I think, going to need a reasonably sized and sophisticated workshop. Need a knowledge of mechanisms and how to build. You may also need somewhere to trial them.'

'If you were trialling them, would you build up mock devices?' asked Macleod.

'Well, think about it,' said David. 'According to what you've said—and sorry, I find this quite horrific—they took a man working on a roof and effectively blew him off into an alleyway. You've told me he's made the man land in front of a couple. You've got to work at this to get a rough idea of the weight of the man, the explosion that's going to happen underneath. There are the parts to build for it. You're going to have to remotely—or in some other way—activate it. There's a lot gone into this,' said David. 'This is not some random have-a-go numpty. This is somebody who knows their craft.'

'They also have to be capable of tailing someone. Know how people work,' said Macleod.

'I can't speak to that,' said David. 'I can only speak to the side you've talked about with the machines. Whether somebody like that could work with people . . .'

'In your experience,' said Susan. 'Because you will know people who can deal with machines like this. Are they "people people"? Are they somebody who understands people as well?'

'Well, we're not all eggheads stuck away in the dark, scared to come out and into the light,' said David. 'But most of us would rather be at home in a workshop than with people.'

'So could they have somebody else working with them?'

'You're going above my league here,' said David. 'I don't think I could do what you've said when it comes to the people, but that's just me.'

'Be candid with me,' said Macleod. 'How many people in Scotland could do this?'

'To have the inclination, the time, and the facilities? I don't think so. I mean, it's difficult. Could I build these machines? Well, maybe. But you'd have to have some experience. You'd have to have a lot of working time with them. I get the mechanisms, having seen them built, what you've explained. But to actually finesse them, to actually make them work exactly how you want. You need the experience,' said David, 'or you need a heck of a lot of trialling.'

'So,' said Macleod, 'you would need someone who maybe even worked on them first time round.'

'Working on them first time round would be great. You said it came from a film. Who was it that worked on it first time round?'

'Stephen Fitz,' said Susan.

'Fitz! I know the name, but my, that is a while ago. Inspector, I'm only forty. I wasn't alive when this film was made.'

'I want you to work with DC Susan Cunningham,' said Macleod. 'Devote your time to her. Go with her. Do whatever she asks.'

'I do have courses to run.'

'We'll cover the financial side. You need to spend time away from your college work. You need to give me the time on this,' said Macleod. 'I'll be candid with you. I need to find this killer, and I need to find him fast. This machinery is our best link. We don't understand it. Susan can try to understand the person. We can try to understand anybody working with them. But I need someone who understands the type of person who would build this and how they would do it. I think you're our best bet.'

'So please,' said Susan, 'get somebody to cover you. Cancel whatever. If you need me to talk to whoever employs you, not a problem.'

'Put them to me,' said Macleod. 'Not to Susan. Put them to me. My name's known and Susan and you need to focus, not deal with agitated bosses.'

'Well, there it is,' said David. 'Looks like I'm on the team.'

'Good,' said Macleod. 'Susan will direct you. See what the two of you can come up with. I'm happy for you to work away at your own business in the free time outside of this, but this takes priority. Be prepared to come at the drop of a hat.'

'Okay,' said David. 'I warn you, I'm not very good at going into scenes of—'

'You're a civilian, so to speak. Well, we will not let you walk into something that you really are going to struggle to see. You'll see the devices, but you won't see them with any victims. We'll clean that side of things up.'

'Thank you,' he said. 'I'll do my best.'

As they made their way back in the car, Susan turned to Macleod.

'You're putting a lot on him, aren't you?'

'No,' said Macleod, 'I'm putting a lot on you. Find me this person. Steer Mr Bairstow. Help him but challenge him. He's here to work for us now,' said Macleod, 'and we're going to need him. Understand what he knows. Learn as much as you can. You're going to be our go-to person for these machines.

And I think you're up for it. And I think you're capable,' said Macleod.

He saw the smile and the confidence being built up inside her. But it was going to be a fragile confidence, he knew. You don't have something happen to you like losing a leg without having the house becoming shaky and potentially ready to fall down around you.

Chapter 14

A little green sports car drove over the Severn Bridge, then raced along the south of Wales, heading for Tenby. Sophie Sallerson had been the star of the film. Only a teenager then, now, some sixty years on, she was just touching her eighties. Clarissa wondered what she would find.

All the reports she'd read recently around the actress said she was more of a recluse than a showbiz star. Indeed, it had been hard to find her address, because she'd been keeping it from the public. Clarissa had to use her rank, saying who she was, when she spoke to the woman's agent to get an address just outside of Tenby.

The Welsh coast was today in glorious sunshine, as the wind blew through her hair crossing the Severn Bridge, the water vanishing quickly down below. Patterson seemed relaxed too, embracing the wind. She wondered if Pats was becoming far too used to it.

Previously, he'd sat almost in abject terror, hanging on for his life. Of course he said nothing. Pats didn't. But now, still wearing the large cravat that covered the cut on his neck, he almost seemed at peace in the car. Clarissa was worried that her driving had slowed down. Nobody sat at peace in this car.

'How much further?' asked Patterson.

'Something like thirty or fifty miles.'

Patterson sat back in the car. 'And so, she's going to be, what, in her seventies?'

'Yes,' said Clarissa. 'She did little later on in life, but she was an active actress for a good while. The part got her notoriety, but, well, it was different. Not the best way to be known. Especially back then when things were more wholesome, at least on the surface.'

Eventually, they pulled up in front of a modest but quaint house on the cliffs near Tenby. The view was stunning out into the Bristol Channel, and the sun shone down reflecting on the sea. There was a light wind blowing, and Clarissa, although always desperate for the Highlands, could see why someone would retire here. It was remote enough. Tenby was nearby, but there was a seclusion with it.

She parked up the little sports car, climbed out, and was about to make her way to the door when it opened. A woman dressed in bright green trousers and an orange top almost skipped across, belying her age.

'Now that's delightful,' said the woman. 'Look at it. You must take me for a spin.'

'Well, if I've time,' said Clarissa. 'I'm Detective Inspector Clarissa Urquhart. This is Detective Constable Patterson. We're here to talk to you about the *Slaughterhouse* film,'

'Of course, of course,' said the woman, but she was over at the car looking inside of it. 'Stunning, absolutely stunning.' She turned to Patterson. 'I bet you love coming out in this car.'

Patterson stood almost motionless. 'It's an experience,' he said; 'undeniably, an experience.'

Clarissa nearly collapsed with laughter. Patterson was really coming into his own, with a fantastically dry sense of humour.

'Could we, Sophie, pop inside,' said Clarissa. 'I'd really like to talk to you about your time on the *Slaughterhouse* film.'

'Of course, darling,' said Sophie, and she turned, walking like someone everyone was watching on a catwalk. Entering the house, Clarissa thought it sweet rather than something that suited a superstar, for Sophie had been a superstar of sorts in her day,

'Could I tempt you to a glass of wine,' said Sophie. 'I've a bottle open.'

'I'm afraid I'm on duty,' said Clarissa; 'otherwise, I'd absolutely love to. I've got to set out an example for my younger partner.'

Patterson raised an eyebrow, and Clarissa shook her shoulders at him, giving a 'What else do you think I do?' image.

'Don't mind if I drink, do you? But I understand totally, darling.'

Sophie really came with the feel of a superstar. She talked like you were there to see her. Which ironically, of course, Clarissa was. Just not in an adoring fashion.

'Can you tell me about the crew from the slaughterhouse and your time on it?'

'The crew? Well, what can we say about the crew?'

'Well, let's start with Franz Kahn, because he's alive. Your director. How did you—'

'Franz was difficult,' said Sophie. She raised her hand up to her head as if this was a hard statement to say.

'In what way?' asked Clarissa.

'Did you know nowadays,' said Sophie, 'they have intimacy directors? People who look after how you relate to each other during difficult scenes. Naked scenes, sex scenes, scenarios like that. Just to keep everybody together, you know.'

'So I've heard,' said Clarissa, although Patterson was looking at her as if he'd never heard of it in his life.

'Well, we didn't have those back then. Things were much more robust.'

'You were put under a lot of pressure, were you?'

'An awful lot of pressure, dear. But you had to do it. It was what you did at the time. It was expected of you. Women weren't—well, look at you. You wouldn't have been around then. You certainly wouldn't have been a detective—what did you say?'

'Detective Inspector,' said Clarissa. The woman was accurate, of course. She wouldn't have been a detective inspector back then. She'd have been in the typing pool, probably. And probably investigated for murdering her own boss because he said something she didn't like!

'It toughened you up, doing those sorts of scenes. Some of the men were—well, some men were nice, to be fair,' she said. 'Franz? No. Franz was going to take every bit of you, expose it, right there for the public, to milk their money in. Don't get me wrong; he wasn't after you yourself; he was after what your body could do for the film and launching it. He didn't give a damn about you, though.'

'Where is he? These days,' asked Clarissa.

'He's in a home. He's gaga,' she said. 'Why are you asking?'

'You may not have heard, but in Scotland we've had killings that have occurred in the same way as the killings in the film happened.'

'The press has been getting in touch with my agent. I've told them I don't want to speak to them. I've had enough of all that. In fact, I wouldn't have spoken to you, but obviously, you are the police.'

'Well, thank you,' said Clarissa. 'I wouldn't be asking except we think it may be useful to solving the case.'

'Well, of course,' she said, 'but Franz is gaga. It's not me, either,' she said. 'I live down here in Wales and I have no reason to do it. Besides, did you say they were killing people in the same fashion as the film?'

'Yes.'

'Well, you see, that's the thing. You would need someone who understood all that stuff, the machinery. I suppose it could be the cameraman. Somebody said he was still around. He's not dead.'

Sophie took a gulp of her wine and spun around in dramatic fashion like the detective at the end of the film, ready to reveal the killer.

'Well, I know, we had a grip on the film. And he's not dead— but he's in New Zealand,' she tailed off. 'And I can't see him doing any of that. No, the only person who really understood the machinery was the guy behind it. The machinist. He was the real genius. I can't recall his name. Let me think. Fitz. Stephen Fitz.

'That was it. He was quite the person. The real genius on that film. I mean, yes, I was the star, darling. Of course I was. And I paid for that. Franz made us do some rather dubious things in the film. It wasn't just blood and guts and gore, which back in those days, well, you didn't show it the same. If you did, it got a triple X classification.

'But he wanted nudity along with it. He wanted heavy-handed nudity. Abuse of women, they would say now. It's not a pleasant film. You have seen it, haven't you?' she said.

'I have, and your acting's very good in it,' said Clarissa.

'Marvellous. But I agree, it's very heavy-handed treatment.'

'Do you know I actually got slapped several of those times? Just to make it look more real. You wouldn't get that nowadays. You'd get pulled in for assault. But I have to thank him for it, though. It made my name. I got other parts, better roles. You've seen some of those, I take it.'

'I have,' said Clarissa. 'You really were quite excellent.'

'Well, thank you, darling,' she said. 'You also know there's a grand display planned. At least there was about the machinery.'

'No,' said Clarissa. 'What do you mean?'

'Well, they were going to highlight the props. Do you remember that man in the Sinbad films, Harry Harrison? Well, they were doing tours and that, weren't they, round the different museums to show his ability with puppets and models. Fantastic. Forerunner of many generations.

'But Fitz was going to get a special all about how he made the machines and all the dangerous props. Because the props in those days, they were amazing. But some of the death scenes—quite astonishing how they did them. Of course, Fitz made them so they were non-lethal. That was part of the difficulty, making sure that you would not end up injuring people with it.'

'You said there was going to be some sort of display,' said Patterson suddenly.

'Yes, darling. The recent revival. You know the film's coming back. Well, they asked me to front all that. But I'm not doing it. I'm not doing it because you get all the journalists asking you all the sordid questions about what it was like and who was—well, you know, all that stuff. People need to focus on my later career.'

'Well, of course,' said Patterson. 'But you said it was Fitz . . .'

'Yes. Yes, yes, of course. They were going to highlight the machines and how innovative they were, how ahead of their time. A proper sort of Harry Harrison effort for him. But the studio decided no.'

'Was Fitz alive at that time?' asked Clarissa.

'Yes, I mean this is a year, two years ago now. Maybe it takes time to organise these things, these events. They're planning so far ahead, really.'

'But they decided not to.'

'That's correct. Instead, they decided they wanted to focus on the more controversial sides of the film.'

'The sex and the nudity,' said Patterson.

'Always sells, doesn't it, darling? It's quite disappointing though, isn't it? Even in this generation, when we're talking about everything being much more controlled and done properly, at the heart of it loads of people still want to see the filth. Filth still sells. But it's a better time to be an actor.'

'You said that the director wasn't like that, personally. He was just wanting to put it out there. He didn't come after you in a personal sense?' clarified Clarissa.

'That's what I said, darling. Not that there weren't other figures there who did. I mean I was in my late teens. I played them off against each other. Got what I wanted. I didn't end up with any of them before you spread that rumour anywhere.'

'We're the police and we don't spread rumours,' said Clarissa. 'We're just trying to find out the detail.'

'Of course you are. These male figures, some studio execs. They're all dead now.'

'And you say the machinist is dead.'

'Fitz died. I think he's buried somewhere up in Derbyshire. He was a genius. I didn't know him well, but he was a genius.

They did him wrong, I will say that. They didn't do right by him. Which is a pity because he deserved better.'

'Well, thank you,' said Clarissa.

'Do I get a ride in that car now? That fabulous car?'

'Stay here a bit, Pats, will you?' said Clarissa.

Over the next hour and a half, Clarissa drove the older lady around. By the time she dropped her back, she'd clarified the story, making her go over it three times without letting her know she was going over it. It all checked out.

'What have we learned?' asked Patterson getting into the car after Sophie had returned to her house.

'What we've learned is that we have got nobody in the frame. Our cameraman doesn't work for me. They're all so old. We've got a gaga director in a home. Sophie isn't capable, an aging alcoholic. Besides her, why would the director be doing it? Pointless. And we've got a grip in New Zealand somewhere. Otherwise, everybody seems to be dead.'

'So, what do we do?'

'We call Macleod.'

Ten minutes later, Clarissa pulled over into a lay-by to speak to Macleod.

'She's definitely out of the picture? You don't see her as—'

'Seoras, you've got to see this woman. She's a quintessential actress who's now got nothing to do. I don't think she could hold it together. She drinks too much. She doesn't understand mechanisms. I'm struggling to find anyone on the cast.'

'But the idea of the tour being changed,' said Macleod, 'that interests me.'

'Of course,' said Clarissa. 'And if he was alive, I would race over to Fitz and I would interview him, taking him up as a potential prime suspect, or any of his sons.'

'What about his sons?'

'He doesn't have any,' said Clarissa. 'Already checked that. He doesn't have any family. A man for his machines.'

'Which means that the slight would have been even more. He really would have been hit by it.'

'He's dead, Seoras,' said Clarissa.

'So following up, where else do we go?' asked Macleod.

'We have got nowhere. You told me to chase through the film side of this. Well, the film side of this says that the person who would have been most upset would have been the machinist.'

'Okay, so follow it up. Even if he's dead, find him. Make sure he's in that grave. Make sure that anybody else attached to him wouldn't have a vendetta. Did he have a carer, a special friend, a lover, somebody who would give a damn about him,' said Macleod, 'enough to carry out killings.'

'I will do,' said Clarissa, 'but to be honest, I think we're barking up a dead end here.'

'Just keep going,' said Macleod. 'And by the way, that's a rubbish pun!'

Interlude 6

It's the preparation that makes the difference. You make the scale models. You work it out. An initial idea is just that, and you have to sketch it down on paper. But we have to sketch it down so far away from everyone else.

Then you have to build your models. I always loved building models. Those initial ideas you scale back. You work out your weights. You work out the distances. That's the quiet bit. Working in the darkness, away from everyone. On film sets, it's the same. Before you even arrive on set, you build the models. You stare and think. Everything is quiet. Some of the best moments. Just letting your mind work through the problem. Letting your mind deal with it.

We must build with no one seeing, though. In the film industry, we would build it sometimes through the night. The actors never got to see it. The actors never get to see any of it. However, they got to see the big bang. They got to see it when it suddenly did what it was meant to do.

That's the thing about the machines. They're not grandiose. Most of them are hidden. Hidden away until they're needed. But when they're needed, they come in with a bang. They come in with a terrific explosion of sound, or a sudden explosion of energy that drives something magical.

We also have to make sure that the safeties are working. In the film, you make sure the safeties are working, so we don't injure anyone. But now, now they have to be there in case we have to abort. Cut short in the last seconds so we don't give the machines away. The challenge is the same. Or maybe the challenge is even more difficult. We built in the quiet on the set because it was easier without people around. Now we build quietly so nobody knows what's coming.

Chapter 15

Ross sat in front of his computer collating the CCTV footage from around the alley where the murder had taken place. He had found images stretching back over a month. Something was bugging him when he watched them.

There was a car repeatedly pulling up on the street and a man approaching the house that the machine had been in. He would come to the house with canvas bags, his face covered subtly, whether it be with a hood or maybe a hat that was pulled well down. He was clearly aware of where the camera was, because he wouldn't look towards it. There were no clear pictures. He would carry in oil or other containers, but never enough to get anyone asking questions. It was subtle.

Sometimes in a day, several trips were made. He had a workman's look about him, and that was no lie. For a workman he was, but he wasn't fixing anything. He was building. The canvas bags at times were long, but never ridiculous. That was the genius of it, thought Ross. The mask he wore was perfect.

Ross made a note of the car registration and the colour. He widened out the search to see if he could see where the car had travelled.

He was in his element now. This is what Ross liked. Solid detective work, chasing down the leads. You didn't have to deal with the public here. All you did was work with the images in front of you. They couldn't lie or be deceitful. He also had a good idea how long it would take him to get through the evidence.

That was the thing. You never knew speaking to people how long it would take. Where to begin? Where else would they go with it? Maybe they wanted to discuss something or talk ad nauseam. Maybe it would take you a while to pull out the information from them.

CCTV cameras were different. You knew what they were saying and when they were saying it. Ross checked through the rest of the CCTV and found the car in previous footage around the city. He clocked it beside a warehouse located downtown in Inverness, hidden behind a couple of streets. He wasn't sure exactly what it was for, but it was definitely a warehouse of some sort. Ross picked up the phone, calling Hope.

'What have you got, Alan?' she asked.

'Well, I've got a car that kept stopping outside. I've checked the registration, and the registration is wrong. It's not coming up anywhere, so they've got false plates on it. Likelihood is the car's no longer in existence. They've stripped it down or burnt it somewhere. So, all we have is that car located beside a warehouse. And it happened several times. I think we know where he's going.'

'Excellent,' said Hope. 'Did you find him anywhere else?'

'No,' said Ross. 'Just that warehouse. Back and forward from it. Maybe that's the only time he used the car.'

'Okay,' said Hope. 'But we need to follow that up. Check that warehouse out. I'll tell Macleod.'

Ross sat back down. There would have been a time when he'd have wanted to follow that up. Gone to check out his assumption himself, but not now. *Maybe if he kept working he could get home a little earlier tonight. He'd get to see his boy before he went to bed. Maybe they could even get this case wrapped up. Macleod would go out though,* thought Ross. *At least he was on the case now. He was thorough. And I'm back doing what I love to do. There was a good side.*

* * *

Macleod fielded the call from Hope.

'I think we've got something. Ross has been on the CCTV. Looks like the car that was used to come to the house and deliver the machine was also seen outside a warehouse in the town.'

'Really?' asked Macleod. 'Is there CCTV outside this warehouse?'

'In the street. Ross has clocked the car parking outside this warehouse.'

'What size is the warehouse?'

'It's big enough. You could fit plenty of machinery in it.'

'Well, our man at the college said that's what they needed.'

'Shall I get a team down?' asked Hope.

'No, I'm just driving with Susan at the moment. We'll give it a look. We don't want to all race down just in case we scare them off.'

'Okay,' said Hope. 'Give me a shout. See how you're getting on.'

Macleod drove past with Susan Cunningham and stopped the car just across from the warehouse. There was nobody there. He sat and wondered about it.

'What's up?' asked Susan.

'Well, the thing that gets me is it's just there, the warehouse. Why don't we wait and see? Rather than run in, in case he's not there, we should sit and wait on it. Give it a day or so.'

'You think that's wise,' said Susan. 'Not to enter right away.'

'If he's not in there and suddenly we take away his base of operations, all we've done is put him on the run to a place where we can't find him. Here, we sit and watch it. We can haul him in as soon as he turns up.'

Macleod called Hope, and she suggested Perry watched the warehouse.

It was a day later when Perry reported no one had been seen at the warehouse. Macleod told him to drive off, saying that he would come down with a team.

'What sort of team, Seoras?' asked Hope.

'The sort that can look after themselves. I'll take Susan with me, but we'll have a team who can grab him if he's there.'

'Why Susan?'

'Because, Hope, she's been looking into these machines. I want someone who could recognise them.'

'Fair enough,' said Hope. 'Just be careful. We got set up last time. We could get set up again.'

'I am aware,' said Macleod. Together with the team, Macleod made his way down to the warehouse. He briefed those who were going to be coming in with guns afterwards to snatch the man if he was there. But they were to wait outside. If nobody was inside, Macleod didn't want everything getting contaminated before forensics got inside.

Susan Cunnigham hopped out of the car on her crutches and then followed Macleod across the road as they went to the front door of the warehouse. Macleod pushed at it. Finding it open, he called inside for anyone. There was silence. Slowly, he entered, Cunningham following him.

'I'm not sure about this, Seoras,' said Susan. As they entered a long warehouse, they saw several machines sitting around.

'What are you not getting?' asked Macleod. 'Look at those machines there. Plenty of them, all doing different things.'

'Yes, but I'm not recognising any of them. I know I've only been talking to our man up at the college for a day or so, but I believe I would recognise the odd machine. Don't recognise any of these.'

Susan took out her phone and began to photograph. After taking several photographs, she sent them in a message to David, their contact at the college.

'They just don't look right to me, Seoras. Really.'

'It's a machine. All machines. I mean, they've got bits to imprint, to press, as far as I can see,' said Macleod, 'though I don't know what they do.'

'David will soon tell us,' said Susan. As the pair continued to walk round the warehouse, it felt cold and a little damp. Something was bugging Macleod.

'When you work, Susan, do you need coffee?'

'What do you mean?' asked Susan.

'When you work, do you need coffee? I need coffee. That mug needs to be sitting there when I'm thinking. Sometimes I don't drink it, sometimes it goes cold, but it needs to be there. Perry, when he worked with me, always needed his cigarettes. You could be guaranteed to know if Perry had been working because the cigarette butts were all in the ashtray.'

'What's your point?' asked Susan.

'Spotless warehouse.'

'Well, maybe he keeps it clean because if we came in and he had cups, we could tie him in with the DNA.'

'If he's been working in here, he's bound to have dropped hairs or something. We'd be able to find him.'

'We weren't meant to find him, though, were we? That wasn't the plan.'

'I don't know,' murmured Macleod. 'I don't know. Are we being led a merry dance? Think about it. We have the alleyway. You have the machine left in the roof void.'

'Well, they couldn't very well take it away with them, could they?'

'You could destroy it,' said Macleod. 'You could make it untraceable.'

'You could, but he didn't.'

'No, he didn't, Susan. That tells me he's proud of them. That tells me he wants it to be there. To be taken for posterity. This is the machine that did this. This is the one who killed that man. And it's just like something built in the film, maybe as good as in the film. I don't know exactly how it works at the moment.'

'Well, you'll know soon enough.'

Susan was standing, assessing a message, as Macleod noticed her concentration taken off the rest of the building.

'What's that?' he asked.

'David's come back to me. He's saying that these machines, a lot of them, are just from manufacturing. Used in clothes manufacture, a lot of them. They're not the sort of thing we would use.'

Macleod looked around him and he wondered. 'That seems

strange. Who owned it then? Who owned this place?'

'Well, when I looked it up previously, the old owner died years and years ago. This place had been abandoned.'

'Well, I'm not one hundred per cent convinced of it,' said Macleod. He stopped and looked here and there. Then he disappeared down a small corridor before finding a toilet. He looked inside it.

'Nothing's been used,' said Macleod loudly. 'Nothing's been used, Susan. A toilet. No matter how well you clean a toilet, it'll still look used if it's been used. You might get that initial shine but why? Why would you be bothered about cleaning it? As long as you clean it enough that it's hygienic. If this guy is more interested in his motors . . .'

There was a sudden silence from Macleod. Susan looked over at him. 'You okay?'

'No,' said Macleod. 'No!' Suddenly, it was like a fear gripped him. Macleod reached forward, grabbing Susan and sweeping her up off her feet. Her sticks flailed wildly.

'Lose them,' said Macleod.

'Why?' asked Susan.

But Macleod was already running with her. Carrying her made it very difficult and he felt like he was stumbling left and right. As he got to the door at the front, Susan clattered into it first, smacking her head off it, causing her to yelp. However, Macleod drove on through with her, and ended up stumbling outside the building. He tried to get to his feet, picking her up again, and took another couple of steps. He was blown off his feet by an explosion behind him that took out every window in the warehouse, and brought on a sudden collapse.

Lying on the ground outside, Macleod felt a trickle of blood running down his nose. The explosion had dropped him, his head banging off the tarmac. He looked over at Susan. She was lying on the ground, and rolling away. She stopped and looked at him.

'Are you okay?' he asked.

'I think so,' said Susan. 'I truly hope so.'

Macleod then looked up across the street. To his disgust, he saw a line of about ten press people, some with cameras, some there clearly for the live action.

'I hate these vultures,' he said. He hauled himself to his feet and walked over to Susan Cunningham. He went to scoop her up in his arms. She told him not to.

'I can't have you carrying me. You're the boss,' said Susan. 'Let me put my arm around you. I'll hop somewhere clear.'

'Not one of them is coming to see if we're all right. They're just filming it. I'm going to . . .'

'Just help me,' said Susan.

Macleod picked her up and let her hang on to his shoulder as she hopped along on one foot. As they got clear, Macleod picked up his phone and dialled in.

'Just in case you've heard, the recent demise of me is a lie and I'm still good to go. Get the cleaning units in as quick as you can. We need to be back up and running.' Macleod put the phone down. He turned and glared at the assembled press but they didn't care. They just took more and more photographs, happy to watch the misery out on the streets.

Chapter 16

Macleod stood looking out the window of Hope's office. It had once been his own, and the view had always been a comfort. Today he was edgy, though. Thankfully, he didn't have to look out of his office, because he would have seen the press at the front of the building, waiting for a story. Macleod was in the paper. Right in the front. Someone had caught a picture of the building behind him exploding, and he racing forward, Susan Cunningham in his arms, tumbling out of the building onto the ground.

He'd been told by the ACC. Perry said it didn't look that bad, but Macleod was furious. They'd been played, walked into it, and he hadn't seen it coming. He thought he'd done the right thing. He'd had Perry watch the building. No one had come, but somehow, they knew. Somehow, they'd had the patience.

It made sense, of course. If you were a machinist making such things that needed to go right the first time, you had to have patience to go through the many iterations before you got it right. Macleod needed to come at this from another angle. However, he was currently waiting for Clarissa to join the call. She was on the move, but she would stop off before making her way the following day into Derbyshire, looking for the burial site of Stephen Fitz.

'Seoras,' said Hope. 'She's on.'

Macleod nodded without looking back. He drew in a breath. It had been a while since he'd been fully in charge. What he didn't like about this was it wasn't run of the mill. He'd been brought in, not goaded but procured. It had been set up. He was the master, apparently. The master detective though he thought nothing of himself in that regard.

If he became arrogant, he missed it—he missed everything. His team was battered and bruised. Cunningham missing part of her leg, Patterson only just getting back into action, Ross not himself, Clarissa only having stepped up. Was he ring-rusty too?

No, you didn't lose it. He could feel the chase beginning; he could feel the appetite growing. He'd find this man; he'd find this person who was doing this. Losing the grimace that was on his face as he stared out, and instead putting on what he thought was a nondescript visage, Macleod turned. 'You're here to join us,' he said to the screen on the wall.

'We've only just arrived. On the bright side,' said Clarissa, 'I didn't need somebody else to set it up for me.'

The barbs are there. At least she's in excellent form, thought Macleod.

'What do we actually have?' asked Macleod. 'What do we actually have? What do we know about our killer?'

'He needs a machine warehouse, somewhere to build his devices and the skill to build them,' said Susan.

'He also needs somebody else probably,' said Ross. 'Needs somebody to play a different role for him.'

'Do we know of their age?' asked Macleod.

'No,' said Perry. 'But if there's two of them, there could be one old, one young.'

'What else do we know about him?'

'Well,' said Susan. 'He likes to play people along. He likes the attention.'

'Or he's missing attention,' said Perry. 'Maybe he wants the attention. Maybe he thinks he deserves the attention.'

'How far out from Inverness could this man be, Ross?' asked Macleod. 'You've seen him driving about.'

'But we haven't been able to identify him with a building except the one he wanted us to,' said Ross. 'I think we should be very careful following any leads.'

'Absolutely,' said Macleod. 'But where could he be?'

'Well, we know he's mobile in a car. He may have a different one. So, he could be anywhere within driving distance.'

'But the attacks are taking place within Inverness,' said Perry.

'So, we're looking for someone who could drive anything up to three or four hundred miles away. Would you be that far away?' asked Macleod.

'Might make procurement easier,' said Hope.

'What about getting the stuff?' ask Macleod. 'Is there any way we could . . .?'

'Well, I talked about this with David up at the college,' said Susan. 'There are not that many pieces of the kit that are, how would you put it, very specialist in design. Just about everything's made of what would be bog standard pieces. You could buy them from many places, especially if he's got his car to travel.'

'He doesn't seem like the person who's going to have an account,' said Perry. 'They've been brilliant so far.'

'What about the technical stuff?' said Macleod.

'David had a look at both devices, said Susan. 'He said that absolutely both of them had all the critical bits self-built. He said there wasn't anything in there that he could buy off the shelf and he could trace because they were basic mass-produced bits. And if there was anything, he'd removed all the identifying parts.'

'It's to be expected,' said Hope. 'After all, he's building these things. He must understand how you get them.'

'So, what have we got,' said Macleod. 'How do we go after this guy? We're chasing down the machinery route, but we have brought nothing in from there yet. What about you, Clarissa?'

'All I've got are dead people,' she said. 'I'm drawing a blank now. We're following through and checking up. We're making sure everything that's been said is right regarding those remaining crew and cast members. I have found nobody that's capable of doing this, or even been anywhere near Inverness to do it.'

'What about the studio?' asked Susan. 'The studio could just . . .'

'No,' said Macleod. 'No, not the studio. It's two. If the studio was doing this, you would have many more people involved,' said Macleod. 'They'd be paying somebody to do it. At the moment, this is too personal. It's done too well.'

'The studio, anyway,' said Clarissa, 'went down the lines of trying to promote the film using all the censorship that went on around it. Not the technical expertise. They poo-pooed that.'

'And the man that built the machines,' said Patterson, 'is now dead. The one person who had a problem with it isn't here. And he's got no kin. We're going to try to check if he's got any friends that might have taken up the gauntlet.'

'They'd have to be technically adept friends,' said Susan. 'David says this is top-notch; this is somebody on the top of the game.'

'So,' said Macleod, 'it absolutely fits Mr Fitz. Unfortunately, Mr Fitz is six feet under.'

'Are we being played along those lines as well?' asked Hope.

Macleod raised his shoulders to show he didn't know.

'Well, I suggest, Seoras,' said Hope, 'we go back to some boring work by combing the areas outside of Inverness for warehouses large enough, and then checking them for machinery. But we do it on the quiet.'

'Absolutely,' said Macleod. 'I think you're right. And totally on the quiet. The killer's expecting us to follow the clues left. We're still getting these envelopes. It's all like the film. The thing is, next time we're looking for a circus act.'

'Circus is three weeks from coming to town,' said Perry. 'I checked.'

'That doesn't mean there won't be any circus act,' said Macleod. 'Either that, or it means we've got a three-week stay of execution. However, the film's about to get its re-release opening.'

'You think something will happen then?' asked Clarissa.

'If you want to make the maximum impact you can from it, when would you do it?' said Macleod.

'If you want my opinion,' said Perry, 'it feels to me like a fan of the previous work. Either that or the original constructor. There's definitely a highlight on the devices. Even the bomb—there was skill and an art in it.'

'I got word from Jona,' said Hope. 'It's not even a bomb-bomb.'

'A bomb-bomb,' said Clarissa. 'I didn't know there were such technical niches.'

Hope gave her a wry smile. 'It wasn't a proper explosion. Apparently, if you'd been inside, you'd have been all right,' said Hope.

'It didn't feel like that when everything was blowing up,' said Macleod.

'No, it didn't,' confirmed Susan.

'Nothing deadly was inside. The windows blew out, doors blew out, because the explosive elements were there along those fixtures. It gave the impression of an enormous explosion, like a proper bomb, but it wasn't a bomb,' said Hope.

'He's kept you alive,' said Perry. 'I suppose that's something you can be happy with.'

'Be happy with?' said Macleod.

'Well, he intends to keep you alive at least until the last murder, which is you.'

Everyone else suddenly stared at Perry.

'What?' said Perry. 'That's exactly what's happening. He will not go for Seoras until he's ready.'

'So, what are you suggesting,' asked Macleod. 'That I'm the one who goes and does all our public investigating? Because we know at the very least, he will not blow me up.'

'Actually has some merit, doesn't it?' said Perry.

'We've tried coming at this from two different angles,' said Macleod. 'We've tried pushing along distinct lines. Traditional route, we're getting dragged in. Going down the film route, we're just not getting anywhere. So maybe the old-fashioned spadework is what we need. Go for the detail; find the warehouse.'

'We'll get somebody on to search it then,' said Hope. 'You're on the quiet, Ross,' she said suddenly. 'Organise it. Take charge of that. You're good with maps, details, sizes. Organise it. Do it on your own. No other people involved. You run that.'

Ross nodded.

'In the meantime,' said Macleod, 'let's try and not get ourselves killed. Let's watch what we follow with the lines of enquiry. And let's not race into any buildings—unless you're with me, according to Perry.'

'I'll check and see if there's any other circus acts coming,' said Perry. 'I haven't seen any, but that doesn't mean smaller outfits couldn't be looking to do things. Church gatherings, fetes, stuff like that.'

'All of it,' said Macleod. 'Get on top of all of it.'

'But also,' said Perry, 'I don't think I'm wrong about the constructor.'

'Well, unless somebody's doing a proper magic act of bringing him back from the dead,' said Clarissa, 'you're out of luck.'

'You might laugh at me for this one,' said Perry, 'but make sure he's dead.'

'You want me to exhume him,' said Clarissa.

'Yes,' said Macleod. 'If there's evidence to say he might not be dead, absolutely. Just make sure the press aren't watching.'

'Trust me, if I'm digging up a grave, it's going to be done on the quiet,' said Clarissa. 'Either that or Patterson's doing it.'

It was a small one, but it caused a chortle in the team, one that Macleod thought was good. The case was dragging a lot of them down, none more so than Ross. He even felt bad, having been the one who had used the CCTV to find where the car had gone. Macleod had told him not to be. After all, it was Macleod who decided to go in. It was Macleod who ran the whole operation. But Macleod thought Ross was disappointed.

Macleod was coming back, and if he was successful, maybe Ross thought he would come back permanently. Seoras wanted to shake his head at the thought, but too many people were watching him just now.

'We need to double down. Make sure everyone's dead who should be dead. Find anybody who isn't and find out what they're doing. And let's do it quick. I don't buy this. The circus is three weeks away,' said Macleod. 'Something's coming. Something's coming for us. I can feel it. We need to get hold of this guy before he does everything he says he wants to do.'

Macleod suddenly realised that meant him and the end of his life. The quietness of the team showed they understood that as well. The screen went off, Clarissa and Patterson disappearing. The team left Hope's office, leaving Macleod and her behind.

'You can come down and use it if you want. I'll move out to the main office.'

'No,' said Macleod. 'That'll give them the idea that I can step back in here. This was your case. They overreacted.'

'You really mean that?' asked Hope.

'Of course I do.'

'But you're enjoying it, aren't you? You're enjoying being back in the thick of it. I don't mean you're enjoying the deaths, but . . .'

'I know what you mean,' said Macleod. 'Does it really show that much?'

'Only to me,' said Hope. 'Only to me.'

Chapter 17

The little green sports car rumbled through the Derbyshire hills on a day that was colder than it should have been. The wind whipped along and although it was dry, Clarissa was wrapped up well in her shawl.

'I think it's just beyond the next village,' said Patterson.

'Cheers, Pats,' said Clarissa. 'It's funny when you go round looking at graves, isn't it?'

'Why?' asked Patterson.

'You feel you're disturbing the dead. Does it not give you an eerie feeling sometimes?'

Patterson shook his head. He wasn't one to be like that, unlike Clarissa. He was not a superstitious man. She, on the other hand, had seen too many things. She'd heard so many rumours, many legends, and myths working in the art world, that at some point some of them would get to you. Not that she thought they were all real; not that she believed in things that went bump in the night, but she didn't disbelieve in them either.

Some of them were distinct things to be kept away from, not disturbed unless you had to. She didn't have the faith that Macleod had, but she wondered about him as well. If she'd said to him that really he was quite like her in believing mystic and strange things, he'd have corrected her. Wrongly, in her opinion, but he'd have corrected her all the same.

It was funny that, wasn't it? How weird were our beliefs? Indeed, how weird were they? These things raced through her head as she sped up and down through the Derbyshire hills, until they arrived at a graveyard on the side of a hill.

It was a lonely area. As she stepped out of the car, Clarissa could see maybe one or two houses in the vicinity. There was plenty of land. A lot of sheep as well. But there wasn't any large town within sight.

Clarissa wondered why she was looking for the large town. Was it the graveyard that did it? She was used to being out in the open; after all, she was a country girl at heart. But this wasn't her country. There was no heather for a start. It wasn't really moorland either, more farmland. *Oh well,* she thought, *we best get on with it.*

'Come on, Pats,' she said out loud, 'let's go find this guy.'

The two of them stepped inside the graveyard. It wasn't particularly large. Clarissa thought it maybe had fifty headstones at most. She walked slowly around, looking for the headstone of Stephen Fitz.

A lot of the gravestones were ancient, covered with lichen. Some of the stonework was worn away, so you could barely make out any of the lettering on it. However, the gravestone of Stephen Fitz was soon found. It was quite clear—new, white marble. Clarissa sat down on her haunches, bringing her head level with it, and found Patterson joining her.

'There he is,' said Patterson.

'No,' said Clarissa. 'There is the headstone.' Patterson eyed her up.

'What was Perry saying?' said Clarissa. 'Macleod too. We need to make sure that Stephen Fitz is in there.'

'And how are we going to do that?'

'Paperwork, Pats, paperwork, and people who actually were here.'

She stood up and looked around. There was a small hut on the far side of the graveyard and Clarissa could see there was a fresh grave being dug over in the far corner. Somebody must be about.

She stood back up, marched across to the little hut, banging on the side of it. There was a moan from inside, and a disgruntled man made his way out of the front door. He turned on seeing her, and stopped in his tracks.

'You from Scotland?' he asked.

It was maybe the tartan trews, the tartan shawl, or just the wild look in her eye that must have given it away to him.

'I am indeed. I'm Detective Inspector Clarissa Urquhart with Police Scotland. This is Detective Constable Patterson. We're trying to trace someone by the name of Stephen Fitz. I believe he's in one of the graves over there.'

'Well, he's not going to run too far then, is he?' said the man.

Clarissa gave a wry smile. 'I want to know that it's him in there.'

'Really?' said the man. 'That could be difficult. I'm not good at putting people back together.'

'Back together,' said Clarissa.

'There's not a coffin in there. He was cremated. Small casket. So, I dug a hole, and he buried a small casket in there.'

'How many were here for it? The funeral.'

'Mother wasn't,' said the man. 'One person.'

'Do you remember what they looked like?' asked Clarissa.

'Well, they were fairly young. A lot younger than you and me, anyway.'

'Twenties, thirties, forties?'

'One of the lower ones,' said the man.

'What colour of hair did he have?' asked Patterson.

'He had a hat. Bobble hat. Green, I think,' said the man.

'How would you describe his face?' asked Clarissa.

'Nondescript.'

Clarissa did her best not to look annoyed, but she could feel her right hand tensing. She wanted to slap the man and tell him to get a grip. But when she looked at him, she didn't feel he was being obstructive. He just wasn't one of those people who remembered things. And if it was several months ago, maybe he didn't.

'So, they came along, and what?'

'Well, I dug the hole for them. I left them. They put it in, they covered it up as best they could, and I filled in the last bit and made it neat and tidy.'

'Did you see the casket he put in?'

'No,' said the gravedigger. 'He said he wanted to be alone for a quiet time.'

'Is there any sort of paperwork involved?' asked Patterson.

'Of course, I've got it in the office here somewhere. Although a lot of it's scanned onto computers. I think the original might be here.'

The man toddled off back to the hut. Clarissa looked at Patterson. He gave a sort of nod of the head. As if showing he wasn't quite convinced of what was going on and that there may be an issue. Well, he was several streets behind Clarissa. She was convinced there was an issue here. She did not like the sound of it at all.

The man came out with the paperwork inside a folder. Clarissa took out her phone, took a photograph of the paperwork, and thanked the man. He then returned back inside the hut and didn't emerge again.

'What now?' asked Patterson.

'Well, Pats, first thing we do is we get back into the car because I think we need to have a chat about something.'

They walked quietly without saying a word. The wind was cool on Clarissa's cheeks, but inside she was heating up, burning to discover something. She sat down in the driver's seat with Patterson beside her.

'Well,' said Patterson, 'we're here.'

'Well, Pats, are you any good with a spade?'

'What?'

'I said, are you any good with a spade? We need to dig that place up.'

'No, no, no. We're not digging anything up,' said Patterson. 'There's no way you're getting me to stick a spade in the ground in there. You need to get an order to do that. We're in England now. We'll have to go to the English courts for it. Get a judge to allow us to do it.'

'Well, that will not happen, will it?' said Clarissa. 'We haven't got enough evidence to convince a judge to dig up a grave.'

'So why is there enough evidence to convince you?' asked Patterson.

'Because, Pats, the thing is, something's going off inside of me. I can tell. Perry was right. Macleod suspected it too. Something's not right. Everything's pointing to the machinist. And yet, conveniently, he dies.'

'Very few people die conveniently,' said Patterson. 'They have it happen to them, as opposed to choose it.'

Clarissa raised her eyebrows at him. 'That's just an obstructive comment,' she said. It wasn't, but she wasn't going to be slowed down. 'We're going to come back tonight.'

'Well, let's not use a spade,' said Patterson. 'If you're determined that we're going to see if there's something in there, let's not use a spade. Get some sort of sharp pole. Something that will go down a good six feet.'

'Why six feet?' said Clarissa? 'It's a casket. You don't dig it that deep.'

'All right. A five-foot pole. Something we can knock in and take out and fill the holes up without looking like we've been in there.'

'You know what? I think I know why I bring you along now. It's ideas like that,' said Clarissa. Patterson shook his head and looked out of the car, as she drove off. The day was getting late, and they needed to purchase a large pole and a mallet.

Later that night, the little green car sped around the same roads. It was now dark, one in the morning, when Clarissa parked the car up. The two of them stepped out into the graveyard, Patterson looking somewhat nervous.

'Just don't hang about,' said Clarissa. 'Come on.' Patterson was carrying a large five-foot pole and Clarissa a mallet. She made a direct line.

'Don't walk there,' said Patterson. 'That's a grave. Show a bit of respect.'

'I'm on the job at the moment,' she said. 'I've got to do this. These people, they will not be bothered.'

'I don't care,' said Patterson. 'Show some respect.' Clarissa sighed and stepped off to one side and walked round, coming to the grave that they wished to test. Patterson pushed the pole in and Clarissa hit the top with a mallet. The sound was significant, but they were out in the middle of nowhere. of absolutely nowhere. The pole descended until there was only about a foot of it left above the ground.

'There's nothing there,' said Clarissa.

'We need to do some more, just in case we missed it.'

Clarissa again shook her head but gave the go-ahead to Patterson. He pulled the pole out, set it up again, and once more they knocked it into the ground. Eight tries later and they'd not connected with anything substantial.

'This makes little sense,' said Clarissa. 'There should be a casket in there.'

'You're right.'

'Well, I think there's only one thing for it. I think we dig the whole thing up.'

'No,' said Patterson. 'We're not doing that.'

'What qualms have we got about it now? I've shown you this is a fraud. Something's going on and we need to deal with it. Go to a judge if you want, but we need to seal this place off and we need to—'

'No, we don't,' said Pats. 'If this is a fraud and we draw attention to the place, they're going to know we're on to them. We're coming at this from a quieter point of view.'

'What are you suggesting, then?' asked Clarissa.

'Let's trace it back. We've got the paperwork. He's meant to be cremated in a casket. Let's go to the crematorium. They had to give them a body, wouldn't they? Chase that route back first, quietly. We can come back later, get Jona in, so we don't disturb any of the forensic side.'

'You're not half daft, do you know that?' said Clarissa. 'We'll do that. We'll do it quietly. Crematorium then—that's the next port of call.'

The following morning, Clarissa was up for breakfast at the small hotel they stayed in. There was a determination on her face, but what impressed her was there was one on Patterson's face as well.

'You're looking flushed this morning,' she said to him.

'I think this is going to work,' he said.

'Well, you're right. It's certainly the right way to go about it.'

Half an hour later, the pair were in the little green car, heading to the crematorium. It was a good hour away, and the day was already underway for them. Clarissa arrived in the office. She could see flustered people trying to work away quietly, but clearly under pressure. She cornered one man, who looked like he might be in charge.

'I'm Detective Inspector Clarissa Urquhart,' she said, pulling out her warrant card and shoving it into his face. 'I'm sorry to disturb you at a busy time, but I need an answer and I need it quick.'

'Give me ten minutes,' said the man. 'I don't want to keep people . . .'

'I said I needed an answer,' and there was a hand on her shoulder.

'It would be best, Inspector, if we gave the man a moment.'

Clarissa turned round. Patterson's face was serious enough for her to stop. 'Ten minutes then,' said Clarissa. She turned back to Patterson. 'Patterson,' she said. 'You better have a good reason for this. You don't interrupt me when I'm full flow like that.'

'Respectfully,' said Patterson. 'It's a crematorium. There are people here who, well, they need to be saying goodbye and that things need to go correctly. They don't get long. Half hour in, half hour out. So, I think we can wait our ten minutes.'

'You're right,' she said. 'Of course you're right.'

She walked past him, her face serious, until she was out of his line of sight. Then she smiled. He was really coming into his own. Really taking shape. It was funny. She almost liked him more than Als, for all his abilities. Patterson was better with the humour than Als, making him a good sparring partner. And he was ready to challenge her which was why she needed him. She had to report to Macleod and she wanted it all to be right before she got to him. Patterson would keep her right.

It was twenty minutes later when Clarissa was handing over the document to the crematorium manager. He was staring at it incomprehensibly.

'It looks like one of ours,' he said. 'Everything's done out properly and if I was out in the street and you said is this one of ours, I'd look at it and say yes.'

'But,' said Clarissa, 'there's a but coming, isn't there?'

The man swept back his hair. It was thin and balding, and he looked like a man under stress. He was now beginning to sweat.

'Just tell us what the problem is,' said Clarissa. 'It might not be your fault, but I need to know what's the deal with this.'

'We didn't do this cremation; we've no record of this.' He got up, turned to his computer, he turned back two minutes later. 'We did other cremations, but not this one. This is for fraud. This is a fraudulent piece of paper.'

'Bingo,' said Clarissa to Patterson. 'Thank you, sir,' she said to the man. 'Let's get the number, get everything else in case we need to ring him back.' Clarissa marched out of the office, outside into the car park, and picked up her phone. She dialled Macleod.

'This is as sure as you can get. The graveside—Fitz isn't in it. There is a staged burial of crematorium ashes. There's nothing in the grave.'

'The crematorium didn't burn him.'

'Confirmed that.'

'And there's nothing in the grave,' said Macleod.

'No,' said Clarissa. There was a silence.

'How do you know there's nothing in the grave? Have you dug a grave up?' asked Macleod.

'No,' said Clarissa. 'We're not that daft. Because we'd ruin all the forensic evidence. We'd also need to get a judge to do that. I'm off territory here down in England. I'm not crazy, Seoras.'

'So how do you know?' he asked.

'We went in the middle of the night and stuck some poles down through the soil. There's nothing metal in there.'

There was a deep breath at the other side. 'Ethics aside,' he said. 'And trust me, there is ethics with this one. Well done.'

'You don't sound that excited.'

'No,' said Macleod. 'I just had another letter. Apparently, we're about to be put into a spin.'

Interlude 7

One of the key things when you want to cause shock and horror is to make sure that it's up front. It's right there. Something so inconspicuous, so innocuous, and yet it turns into something bloody, gory, something they don't see coming.

It has to have a destructive element, brutally destructive. It has to rip things apart. It has to be so horrific and something you can't stop, something you're powerless almost against once it's begun. That point when you realise that if you had seen it earlier, you could have done something about it. That's what gets people. That's what really makes the difference.

Sometimes you have to be so aware, but people aren't. In a circus environment, it's even easier because there's so much going on. People being entertained. They're watching the performer because the performer has got his own sleight of hand that's going on. He's deliberately making sure that they are looking at him, not the surrounding elements. And you can hide your element in amongst them. They don't see it coming. And amongst all the gaudy rags, amongst all the showmanship, suddenly there's something that has no show about it. It's all just fundamentally destructive. It's brutal, it's hard, and it's harsh. Like I say: Destructive elements should be front and centre, and not seen by anyone.

Chapter 18

Mark Magnusson was having a good day. It had been a while since he'd been on tour with the army, and still in his memory was the combat action he'd been involved in. Of course, he didn't talk to anyone about it. That wasn't something you did. Instead, he was having time out, and time out had just got interesting.

He'd been faithfully watching one of the magazine programmes on the TV during the afternoons, one with a rather delightful blonde presenter. Mark had just seen her in the crowd.

Without trying to be too obvious, he'd found out where she'd gone as she met up with her camera crew on the edge of a playing field just outside Inverness. What had surprised him was the large wheel that was there.

It was glamorous, clearly had fireworks that would go off at its edges, and was well over eight feet in diameter. There were handholds and some sort of locking mechanism, and he presumed someone would climb onto it.

Opposite the large wheel was a man talking to everyone. He had a mask on, like one of those Italian plays. Venice was it? Was it Venetian? Mark wasn't sure. However, what he was sure was that the presenter was going to be involved in it.

What was her name? Joy. That was it. Joy Mackenzie. She could only have been about twenty-five, Mark reckoned, but she had such a cheerful disposition. Every time he'd seen her on the telly, she was always laughing through her interviews.

Seeing her in real life, she was actually a good deal thinner. Maybe what they said about TV making you look fatter was true. Not that Joy was a disappointment, just something that Mark had noted.

Joy, however, had disappeared off into a van and now reappeared dressed in a costume that Mark could only think came from the sixties. He looked around for any more information, a little too shy to step up and ask personally. There was a poster for a circus coming to somewhere near here in about three weeks' time. Other than that, there were a few people on cameras and a lighting crew illuminating the wheel.

The man in the mask, however, was wearing a rather jolly outfit and was tossing some knives. He would flick them into the air, catch them by the handle, and then with the point. Then he'd just rapidly juggle them.

He was explaining to the TV man he was going to be throwing the knife, and that Miss Mackenzie need not be worried. He'd done this before. Mark felt slightly apprehensive. The knives looked real, but they couldn't be, could they?

That was the thing, wasn't it? It looked death-defying, but there was no death about it. He looked over at where the man was putting the knives down on a table. On the table was a box. It was maybe half a metre high and half a metre wide. The lid was firmly down, but Mark couldn't see anything that held the lid down. At the back there was some sort of latch mechanism, but it seemed to be a sort of hinge mechanism, but nothing to physically keep the top closed.

He wondered about its purpose. Maybe the man put his knives in there. Maybe that was it, but there didn't seem to be any carry handles.

Joy approached in her sixties' outfit, miniskirt up round her thigh, tight top with a single headband through her hair, which was now swept round behind her. It was long and blonde.

Mark watched as she was briefed by the man with the knives. Mark wondered what it felt like talking to a mask. Could he even see properly out of those slits? Were there slits? Maybe it was one of those masks that you could see through the eyes, but you just couldn't see into them. He surely wasn't blind, was he? That would just be ridiculous.

Mark was ushered to one side by one of the TV camera crew for obviously getting too close. Meanwhile, the man with the knives insisted that the camera crew move out wider. He had a lane of throwing, he said. Mark wondered what he was on about. How wide did this lane go? If he was that inaccurate, could they all be in trouble?

Joy looked nervous, and she turned to the director, a man in his forties. He wasn't taking any nonsense from her. Mark felt bad about this. Was she being forced into this? Maybe that was the thing about being a presenter. They told you what you were doing. You didn't get an option. Mark was always a sucker to protect a woman, and something about her made him move closer.

He was across from the wheel, almost at right angles with it. It wasn't the sturdiest of looking contraptions and he wondered if there was a strong wind would it maybe fall over. It would have to hold Joy. While not the heaviest of women, she was still a person. She would still be a weight to support.

Slowly, Joy allowed herself to be edged forward over towards the large disk. She inspected the handholds. She had some concern about her skirt, and wardrobe were called in. Well, he could understand this. You didn't want to be spinning round and every time your head was at the bottom, your skirt fell down to reveal what was underneath.

Tape was applied. Mark couldn't see where it was applied to, but clearly it would have the job of keeping the skirt in place. *Why was she in this get-up, anyway?* he wondered. Maybe the man had insisted.

Joy suddenly switched on. She went into presenter mode, and the fears that she seemed to have about what she was going to do vanished. For the next ten minutes, the camera did close-up shots. Mark wondered if that meant Joy would be on the wheel for too long.

A small crowd had gathered now, but all were pushed back, except for Mark. He was so far off to the side, apparently, he was in a safe area. Mark was big, which might have been the other issue. He was six foot two, wide and strong. He had been trained to kill, but Mark was a gentle soul at heart. Unhappy to hurt anyone who wasn't the enemy, he only followed his job. And his job was to protect, not to just kill, to murder.

Joy finished her piece to the camera, stepped aside and was seen taking a bottle of water. She drank about half of it and Mark could see she was slightly pale. *Well, she didn't have to do it if she didn't want to,* he thought. *She could always stop.*

She was led by the director up towards the wheel, and the man in the mask came along too. Joy looked over and saw Mark watching, and she gave a smile. Maybe it was a smile she gave to the public, but it quickly faded as she was manoeuvred back against the wheel.

Her hands went up, and she was tightly cuffed, latched on to the wheel. The wheel was then spun as the masked man stood in front of her. As she went past, he reached up and tapped the bonds that held her. Something was said to her, and she nodded before the wheel was stopped with Joy upright on it.

'Let's see if we can take this in one,' said Joy.

'I've got three cameras on you,' said the director. 'You don't normally get three cameras out here, not for a piece like this.'

Suddenly, Joy went back into mode, saying, 'Wish me luck' to the camera. The man in the mask stepped up and spun the wheel gently.

Mark watched it go round and round, the long blonde hair of Joy Mackenzie falling down towards the ground as she spun. Her hairband did only so much to prevent her hair moving. When she spun back up to the top, the hair fell back down round her ears. There was something slightly surreal about it, Mark thought.

Happy that she was spinning correctly, the man in the mask walked back towards the table that held the box and also a small selection of knives. He took the knives, examining them before picking one up in his hands. He turned round and announced the name of the circus. Then he asked Miss Mackenzie if she was ready? He told her not to move and to be brave. Said that he wouldn't harm her. None of his knives would hit her. But he gave out a laugh with it.

Mark thought that strange because the laugh wasn't a jovial one. There was something sinister about it. The man in the mask turned round to the crowd who were there, maybe some twenty people, and told them to cheer and to do a countdown. They started at ten which Mark thought was quite a long while to be waiting. Surely the camera team wouldn't like this.

Ten seconds. It would be too long a snippet for the telly. They'd have to cut that out.

Nine. Mark could see that Joy's face was not the beaming, smiling one that he was looking for. It was almost a grimace, and the mouth held tight. That was fair enough, he guessed.

Eight. The man in the mask juggled the knives.

Seven. He kept them spinning, round and round.

Six. He now caught them and put them inside a belt that he had around his waist.

Five. He turned, his back to Joy, giving a nod out back to the crowd.

Four. The man turned to face Joy again. Mark couldn't tell what his expression was, hidden beneath that mask.

Three. A knife was whipped out of the belt, held by the point, and his left arm was extended, balancing himself, ready to throw.

Two. The knife was drawn out. Mark was bemused as the man in the mask simply ran off. He disappeared off the pitch, out to the side towards trees. There was a murmur in the crowd. What was going on? Joy shouted, but Mark noticed something, and he wasn't sure anybody else was seeing it. The lid of the box was opening. It didn't flip open, more like something motorised, slowly coming up until it was at a ninety-degree angle with the box, and then Mark saw something rising up. It was metal, on the end of a stand.

One. Mark saw something he recognised. A barrel—albeit a short one—of a gun. The barrel was pointed towards the large wheel.

There was an instinct in Mark—or was it training—something that helped him to size up situations. The gun was pointed at Joy. He needed to get her out of there, needed to take action. He tore off from the standing point he was on as the gun continued to rise up. Would it fire? When would it fire? He couldn't wait to find out.

Instead, he jumped up onto the small stage, turned and drove his shoulder hard into the wheel Joy was spinning on. It rocked. The whole fixture bending. Mark pushed hard with his shoulder, getting down low and driving his feet into the stage.

'What are you doing?' shouted the director, but Mark wasn't listening. Instead, the wheel buckled on the hinge where it was fixed. It turned. There was a crack of wood and the wheel tumbled to the ground, driving Joy to the floor. Mark collapsed on the ground as well and as he did so, the air was split with the sound of gunfire.

He didn't move, but one hand went out and continued to hold down the wheel, which was now lying flat, Joy at the bottom. The gunfire ripped into the hillock behind the stage. It lasted for almost twenty seconds and was sprayed from side to side. And then it stopped.

The machine gun slowly lowered down into the box and the lid descended. Mark looked up. The director was in shock, not moving. The cameramen were behind their cameras, film still rolling, but the public had scattered.

Mark got to his knees, and lifted the wheel up to see the woman underneath. He wasn't sure of her condition and shouted over to others, telling them to come and help him. Although the gun had disappeared back into the box, they were reluctant to step out onto the stage, so Mark barked at them again, giving them an order.

Two cameramen helped him, and they lifted the wheel,

flimsy as it was, off to one side. Mark then raced over, grabbed the box that the machine gun was in, lifted it off the table, and placed it up against the hillock. If it came up again, it would fire at point blank range into it. With half an eye still on it, he turned back to where the disc had now been flipped over. Joy Mackenzie lay on it.

Her nose was bloody. It must have been smashed into the ground when the wheel fell. There were heavy markings on her face. Mark looked at the rest of her body. He couldn't see blood anywhere else. Just the streaming nose.

'I think you're going to be all right,' he said to Joy Mackenzie. She didn't seem to be quite with it. Maybe it was the knock to the head. Maybe it was the trauma.

'Well, get an ambulance,' said Mark. 'Get them here quick. Did anybody see where that guy went?'

Nobody volunteered an answer. Nobody had gone after him by the looks of it. And Mark couldn't blame them. Why would you want to do any of this, having seen what just happened?

He stared off at the trees, wondering if he should go after the man. But he could be anywhere by now and besides, Mark's shoulder was smarting. He'd done everything without thinking. No, that wasn't right. He'd done everything at an incredible speed, his mind reacting as it was trained to do. And she was alive. *But what was that all about,* he thought.

He glanced at Joy—she was just coming round—and then he looked at the box.

'Take care of her,' he said. 'I'm going to stand guard. I'm a soldier, and that's a weapon, and I don't think anybody else wants to be messing with it.'

Chapter 19

Hope McGrath switched off the phone and then stood and looked around her. The large wheel was sitting at the side of the stage and Joy Mackenzie had been taken to hospital. She was in shock, but Hope saw that there was a large soldier still standing over by the gun mechanism. Hope made her way across to speak to him. It was a delight to do so, for at six feet tall, Hope spoke down to many people.

'Hello, I'm Detective Inspector Hope McGrath. You must be—'

'I'm Mark and I'm a soldier,' he said. 'I was the one who knocked the wheel down.'

'They say that a gun popped up out of that box,' said Hope.

Mark was still standing beside it. 'I thought it best if I stay here with it, as I've got some experience with weapons. I haven't tried to open it again,' he said. 'But if it comes up, I might prevent it from doing any damage. I lifted it and put it here because the last time it came up it pointed straight forward. If it does that this time, it'll shoot straight into the bank.'

'That's good thinking,' said Hope. 'How did you clock it?'

'I guess I was just . . . keeping an open mind. I'm used to

this idea of sentry duty. Used to not getting pulled into the one place like they try to do in the circus. Keep your outlook broad so you miss nothing. Maybe that was it.'

'And how did you come to be here?' asked Hope.

'Not long back from a tour. I was walking along, and I'll be honest, I saw Joy Mackenzie. Seen her on the telly a few times and I thought I'd see what she was doing. I wasn't stalking her or anything,' said the man, half smiling.

'It's a good job you did, by the sounds of it. You're the reason she's alive.'

'She looked like she got a pretty busted-up nose, but I think everything else was intact.'

'She's going to survive. Not that she got hit by anything, except the ground,' said Hope.

'Well, that is good news,' said the man.

'What can you tell me about the person who was meant to be throwing the knives?'

'Young, smaller than me, maybe five-ten or five-eleven. Didn't get to see much else about him. Wearing a mask and a fancy suit, so, to be fair, if he's run off, if he keeps that on, he should be pretty easy to spot.'

'If he keeps it on,' said Hope. 'Well done. Thank you for that. Anything else you could tell me?'

'Not really. I've just stood here since then.'

'Well, if you could continue to stand there. I've got a forensic team on the way. They'll have a firearms expert with them. And I'll need someone who knows how to hunt.'

The man nodded and Hope turned to see a rather irate man, almost jumping up and down. She made her way over to him.

'I need my set back,' he said. 'You can't just cordon off these cameras.'

'Something wrong?' Beside the irate director was Constable Perry, looking as chilled out as ever.

'I was just trying to explain to our director here that having filmed all this, we're going to need all the footage and possibly take his cameras in.'

'I'll send you the footage,' he said.

'It's attempted murder,' said Hope. 'We need to gather our evidence. We can't let you send us the image because it could be doctored.'

'I had nothing to do with it,' he said. 'Why would I?'

'Well, it's probably going to do good for your programme, isn't it?'

'I do actually give a damn about that woman. I'm her director, but we care about her. There's a reason she's front and centre. She can perform and she's got the looks for it.'

'Well, go and help her with her looks. Her nose got pretty smashed up.'

'She's alive, though,' said the director.

'What's the deal with all this? Why are you doing it?' asked Hope.

'Well, the circus is coming to town and with the hype that's been going on around the re-release of *The Slaughterhouse*, we thought this would be quite a good thing to set up. But we were doing it with the circus themselves.'

'Who's here from the circus, then? Other than the man that ran off?' asked Hope.

'We've got the circus owner back there,' said Perry.

'Cameras are not to be touched,' said Hope to the director. 'In fact, none of your gear is to be touched until we get forensics here to go over them. I'll get you back what I can, but the rest of it could be part of a criminal case. So, no!'

Hope made her way over to the circus owner and found Perry in her wake.

'I think I've got everything sorted out,' he said. 'Forensics will be here. We've got a bit of a cordon around everything and I had that military guy watching the gun. I reckon he'd be better at it than me. Told him not to touch anything unless he had to.'

'It's fine, Perry, that's all good. What I want to know is how people do this when we know we've got a serious problem with that film.'

The circus owner was about five-foot-five, which then produced the hilarious situation of Hope looking down at him from a great height.

'What's your name?' asked Hope.

'I'm Joe Lasselle,' said the man, 'and I run the circus behind this. I've actually got to get back for tonight's performance.'

'Where are you at the moment?'

'Perth. I've got to hit the road soon. So, if we can wrap this up.'

'It's not a case of just wrapping it up, sir,' said Hope. 'All that equipment is staying until I've had forensics go over it. But more to the point, who's your knife man?'

'It caught me out as much as anyone else,' said Joe. 'Look, really sorry about it, but she's not dead. In fact, she's barely been hit at all. If that guy hadn't knocked her over, she wouldn't have broken her nose.'

Hope couldn't believe what the man was saying. 'If that guy hadn't knocked her over, she'd be dead.'

'The knife man,' said Perry. 'You told me he was called Alfonso.'

'Yeah, he's Alfonso. He was a young man, early twenties,

quite reclusive. But he ran a really good show. So that's why we took him on. We had an idea that we were going to do something else here, the idea being that this would promote the circus coming up. But it wasn't meant to be the knife act. We were going to send jugglers, clowns, and that. The TV guy, he said different.

'He said because of everything that was going on with the re-release of that *Slaughterhouse* film, the hype and the drama of doing the knives would work really well. He said there's a scene in the film, exactly like this.'

'Exactly like this,' said Hope. 'There's a gun that appears and fires from nowhere. Who put the box there?'

'That was Alfonso. Alfonso set the whole thing up. It's his thing, so I don't interfere, you know? They are performers. They keep their sets safe. Yes, you look into it and check it, but everything he has done has been safe. He's been with us for nearly five months.'

'Five months,' said Hope. 'Where have you been?'

'Came up from England. Leicestershire, Nottinghamshire. Went through Derbyshire as well. We picked him up. I think it was Leicestershire. That's right, the week after we did Derbyshire. And then we made our way up through the country until we eventually got up to here. We've done Glasgow and Edinburgh as well.'

'Do you pay for your acts?' asked Hope.

'Of course we pay our acts,' said Joe.

'How did you pay him?'

'A lot of them have bank transfers, but Alfonso wanted everything done in cash. I don't normally do that, but he was so good, I felt I had to.'

'So, you've set up an exact carbon copy of a film and yet you know we're having trouble with that film. You don't think you were being pretty brave doing that? It's a bold move, at the very least.'

'Sounds like a stupid move to me,' said Perry.

'I didn't know anything about him, okay?' said the man ashamedly.

'Just stay here, Mr Lasselle,' said Hope taking Perry to one side. 'We're going to need to run a manhunt, Perry, for Alfonso. I want you to organise and lead that manhunt. I'd get Susan to do it, but she's off doing her other stuff. Get on to that, Perry. Okay? Make sure Ross knows. He should come out here anyway soon.' Hope turned back to the TV producer.

'That circus owner is saying that you pushed for this, you pushed for the wheel.'

'Yes,' he said. 'Look at the surrounding hype. That's what people want to see. We even agreed to her putting on that sixties' outfit.'

'Apparently,' Hope said, 'that's the same outfit as the woman in the film wears. The one who gets shot while on the spinning wheel. It's also a mechanised shooting.'

The producer hung his head for a while, then he looked up. 'We checked everything. It's a reputable circus. How were we meant to know there was a killer amongst them?'

Indeed, thought Hope. *How do you identify a killer when all they seem to do is normal stuff? Suddenly, he just turns around and produces a box with a gun in it. But another gadget. It's always gadgets. Gadgets here, gadgets there.*

Hope saw that Jona had arrived and, together with a firearms expert, she was over at the box.

'What way are you going to play that?' asked Hope from a distance.

'In a minute,' said Jona, 'we're just finishing off with Mark here.'

Jona came over a few minutes later. 'We're going to get it dismantled. Make sure it's not firing anymore. I've got the team here to do that. I suggest if you want to talk to me, you can do it after that.'

'I can wait,' said Hope. 'Perry can't. He's got a manhunt to organise.'

'I'm on it,' said Perry. He went to step past Hope, and she saw him looking slightly shaky.

'You all right,' said Hope. 'I mean I haven't seen you look like that; you seem jittery today.'

'No cigarettes,' said Perry. 'I'm off the cigarettes, remember?'

'Of course, but if you need one . . .'

'if I need one, I'll smoke ten,' said Perry. 'That's what happens with cigarettes. You smoke, and then you get back in the habit. Habits are hard to break. There's a reason they say that.'

'Just make sure you're not cutting back so much that it's at the expense of your thought process and the way you handle yourself,' said Hope. 'We are under stress at the moment.'

'Do you think?' said Perry, and then he apologised. 'Sorry, that's the lack of cigarettes doing that. I'll get this manhunt organised,' he said. 'I'll keep you advised,'

Hope saw Ross arriving and stepped over to brief him. He then disappeared and began organising uniform to take statements from everyone. Hope then returned to Mark, the tall Squaddy.

'So, you say he wore a mask. Can you tell me anything about it?'

'Like one of those Venetian ones,' said Mark. 'Very strange. You couldn't see past it, though. It had like a net curtain past it or some sort of netting around it. Something to make sure you couldn't see any part of his face.'

Why was that? thought Hope. They would know him at the circus, surely. She called over the circus owner, and before Mark, she questioned him.

'Alfonso, you have got a description of him, haven't you?'

'He was very shy and spent most of his time in that mask. He'd insist on wearing it round the circus. Said it gave him that air. The unknown man, as he used to call himself. Nobody knew who he was.'

'And he took cash? Come on, there's got to be something going off in your head there,' said Hope to the man. She was getting agitated. She couldn't believe they'd set this up.

'When I look back now,' said the circus owner, 'of course. But I didn't know. And I didn't push for this. He pushed for this.' He pointed at the producer.

'Well, when I went down to see the circus,' said the man, 'actually, Alfonso came up to me. Said it would be really good. I then made the connection between the film and it and thought, yes, it would. But Alfonso was the one who said it to me. Alfonso was the one who organised it.'

Played, thought Hope. *They played everybody here, set up a scene, more than that, filmed the scene, so it's there for posterity. The first one was dropped in front of everyone. The second one, explosion in front of two people. Every killing, every reenactment of the film is getting seen by someone. The police traps don't. The large knife at the foot of Susan. That didn't get filmed by someone, but that didn't matter because the police bits are about us.*

Jona came up to Hope. 'We're going to need to get the team on to this device. I'll see what I've got, but at first glance it looks very, very clean. Looks like it was wiped already. Have we got anything that the man who threw the knives might have touched?' asked Yona.

Where are the knives? Hope turned to the circus owner. 'Where are the knives?'

'He went with them,' said Mark from a few feet away. He was lingering, watching.

'Great,' said Hope. 'And I take it he didn't touch the box in the time that you saw.'

'Nope,' said Mark. 'The lid opened on its own, the gun came up on its own.'

These people are too good, said Hope to herself. *Too good.*

She was about to walk off when the TV producer turned to her. 'Can I ask you something?' he said. 'Have you ever thought about doing any television? I have an idea for doing past crimes. To have somebody like yourself presenting would be terrific.'

'Someone with experience,' said Hope. 'I've worked quite a few murder cases now.'

'No,' said the producer. 'Just the face. I mean, we'll tell you what to say. You don't need to bring any knowledge into it. But somebody with a face like yourself, tall with the red hair. You'll look great on the telly.'

Hope wanted to hit him. She'd got to where she was because of her abilities, not because of how she looked. But then again, how you looked was a lot on telly, wasn't it? She shook her head and walked. She'd have to find Perry and see how the manhunt was going.

Chapter 20

'And that's you up to date,' said Macleod.

'I can't believe that they actually did that.'

'No,' said Macleod to Clarissa, 'but they did. People don't think. They're not like us. We're looking for the next death. The TV producer was just looking for a bit of fame, a little advertising. These people we're up against, they're good at getting people to buy into what they need. Getting good at giving them what they want, but also fulfilling their own agenda at the same time.'

'So, this great Alfonso then,' said Clarissa. 'Where is he?'

'Perry's got the lead in the manhunt. Hope's overseeing it as well. I do feel like we're chasing because he wants us to chase,' said Macleod.

'You know, in the film…'

'The film,' said Macleod. 'I know. I have watched the film now.'

'And you know what happens next, don't you? The next death's about the manhunt in the film. That's why he's run off. That's why they've organised it like this. So, you can go after him.'

'I do get that,' said Macleod, 'but that's why you're coming at it from a different angle. I need some success from you, Clarissa,' said Macleod.

'Didn't I find you the lack of a body?' she said suddenly.

'That's not good enough,' said Macleod. 'It's not good enough. You're back on the murder team now.'

'Hey, I didn't ask to be back on the murder team.'

'We don't ask for stuff. This is about preventing deaths. This is about catching a killer. We get on with it.'

'And I have got on with it. Are you disappointed in my work?'

'No, I'm not,' said Macleod. 'I'm just hacked off. I'm getting played. The press is everywhere. And I'm in the middle of this without choosing to be. Hope could have handled this. Hope would have been a better figure.'

'Why?' asked Clarissa.

'Because they wouldn't have known her the same. I'm in this because I'm the superstar, as they like to call me. Well, I'm no superstar. I'm like you, dogged. You get a hunch; you follow it up.'

'You're not quite like me, are you?' she said. 'Yeah, I've got fewer morals. You wouldn't have stuck that pole into the grave, would you?'

'Yes, I would,' said Macleod. 'That's why you're here with me. That's why you're on the team for this.' He heard a sigh down the phone. 'What?' asked Macleod.

'I wanted to go on to the arts, you know.'

'It's got an arts side to it this, hasn't it?'

'It's a film! It's not even a good film. It's a dodgy, sleazy, rubbish film. I mean, there's so much sleazy stuff on celluloid,' she said. 'Don't get me wrong, you know, back in the day there was some great films made. But see when they go off piste, see when they go into all the nasty stuff, and then they all hold it up. I don't like it, Seoras, I don't like it, it's not my kind of film.'

Macleod couldn't believe she was talking about what was her kind of film, as if he was interested.

'You need to find me something,' said Macleod. 'You're going to bust this thing open, not Hope. With all the best will in the world, she's going down the path they want. You're the one coming in from a different angle, the one who's going to blindside them. You're the one that's going to get me this,' said Macleod. 'So, get at it, find it, shake things down, whatever you have to do. Get my—'

'Don't you dare,' said Clarissa. 'You call me a rottweiler and I'll pull you up in front of HR.'

'When did you ever get bothered about HR?' said Macleod. 'And I wasn't going to call you that.'

'What were you going to call me then?'

'My number two. You and Hope, you're my number twos. I need you coming through.'

'Okay,' said Clarissa.

She put the phone down, and Macleod, standing in Hope's office, looked out of the window again. It wasn't his office. Every time he looked, it wasn't his office. It didn't bring him the same comfort. Things weren't the same, but then they wouldn't be, would they?

She's my number two, thought Macleod. *My number two rottweiler.* He gave a grin, and then his face went sullen again. She had to bust this open. She had to.

* * *

'How are we going, Perry?' said Hope, as Perry turned away from the search team.

'We've got plenty of people out, obviously having to do it in such a way that we keep them safe as well. See, we know where he's been. We've got a rough path, but we haven't had a physical spotting yet. We're hoping to flush him out of wherever he is.'

'It's the surrounds of Inverness,' said Hope. 'How far could he have gone?'

'Well, we're out of the edges, by where we started from. He's up going into the hills. He could have fanned out in several directions if he hasn't grabbed a car.'

'Have we had any sightings? I mean, he was wearing rather ridiculous clothing. He'd be bright. He's had a mask on too.'

'Mask got seen,' said Perry. 'A man was seen heading off to the east. He disappeared into a wood. We may have him again. We're just waiting to see what else happens.'

'Okay,' said Hope. 'Do you need a coffee? Are you in the middle of something?'

'I'm fine,' said Perry. 'Let's grab one. Could do with one, especially since I'm not having any cigs.'

'Susan would be proud of you.'

'Detective Constable Perry,' shouted the man from the search team. Perry turned instantly, at almost half a jog, back to the table the man was around with several other people. 'Just had a report come through. There's a guy on the run. I suggest we send units down that way.'

Perry nodded to the sergeant at the desk. 'You got this?' he said to him. The man nodded.

'What's going on?' Hope shouted over.

'Been spotted.'

'I'll get the car,' said Hope. 'Get a location, find out what's happening. We want to be there.'

Hope ran to the car, started it, and brought it up close to where the table Perry was at. She watched him speaking for a moment, then he turned and ran over towards the car. He jumped into the passenger seat.

'Here,' he said, 'he's headed down a track. We should be able to take the car down there. Maybe, what, some twenty minutes out.'

The car was already moving before Perry had finished speaking. 'Well done, Perry,' she said,

'We haven't got him yet,' said Perry.

They raced along, but as they got closer to the location he'd been seen at, a phone call came through to Perry. He took the call, making some notes on a pad of paper. When he finished, Hope said to him, 'What's that, then?'

'He's been cornered down at an old run-down mill by a river. I've got the location here. Come on,' said Perry.

Hope could feel tension, but the excitement was charging through her. They had him. They could actually get one of the bastards who was doing this. Finally, something had broken. Finally, all the hard work. They'd made a mistake,

'We got him, Perry. We got him on the run.'

'So it seems,' said Perry.

Was he missing the cigs? Hope wondered. He didn't seem to have his usual confidence.

She drove the car as quick as she could, eventually heading down a track that they had previously been directed to, and then driving on until she saw a line of police cars. Stepping out, a sergeant recognised her and waved her over. Perry followed.

'In there,' they said. 'He's in there.'

'Any idea if he's armed?' asked Hope.

'Have seen no indications. He's still wearing that mask and the outfit.'

'How did you see him?' asked Perry.

'He came this direction, and then one of the officers was going past and saw him in the building. Just at the front door.'

The sergeant led them forward, but told them to hunker down as they came along the path. From behind a small clump of trees, they looked down to where the mill house was. A river ran past it, but there was a small bridge across.

Hope took the binoculars. There, in the doorway, was their man. He came out, looked left and right, and disappeared back in. About two minutes later, he did the same. It was another four minutes before he did the same again. She handed the binoculars to Perry.

'He's obviously looking for something.'

'Well, I think he's trapped, though. I've got units surrounding this area. We can close in on him. If he bolts from the place, we'll have him.'

'In case he goes quick, we'll go down there.'

'Hang on a minute,' said Perry.

'What?'

'I don't know. I just want to see him come out again.'

Hope watched Perry as he stood. He hunkered down with the binoculars, clearly in pain, bending like this. He maintained the position for the two minutes it took for the man to come out. The man wasn't out for long. When he retreated, Perry put the binoculars down.

'We go get him then,' said Hope. Perry nodded.

They made their way back a short distance, leaving two constables to keep watch with the binoculars.

'We'll move in with a strike team of eight. I'll go across the bridge with Perry. The rest of you will surround the house. We've got wave after wave beyond that as well. We'll go in with the nightsticks, pepper spray. You have the tasers too. We'll shout if we need help. Otherwise, stay on the outside.'

'Keep within visual sight of each other,' said Perry. 'Us too, boss,' he said.

Hope nodded and soon they were making their way down towards the bridge. The eight of them, in a single line, moving amongst the trees, staying as well hidden as they could. As Hope reached the bridge, she couldn't see anybody watching. She stole across quickly, still dressed in her jeans and her leather jacket, a nightstick in her hand. Perry was behind her. He had a taser and a nightstick too.

'We'll call him to come out,' said Hope, 'as we surround him. He won't know what to do.'

Hope walked towards the door that was open at the front of the mill. It was an old stone building, and the windows at the top had no shutters. The day was cool, although it was dry, and an airy breeze blew along to the small valley where the mill was located. Hope crept up to the door.

A sense of the chase was in her. Her heart was beating fast. There was almost a grin. She looked across at Perry. He looked somewhat more flat, less excited, less gee'd up.

'Are you okay?' she asked him quietly. He nodded. Hope called out. 'Alfonso, you're surrounded. This is the police. Time to come out quietly.'

There was no sound.

'He's just peeked out,' said a voice in Hope's ear. It was the constable watching from a distance. 'But he's gone back in again.'

'We go in,' said Hope. 'Ready?' Perry nodded. Hope ran

forward and went to turn in at the front door. She went to race through and suddenly Perry was grabbing her by the shoulder.

'No!' he blurted. 'No!'

'What?' she asked. The nightstick was extended, but Perry was shaking his head.

'Back,' he said. 'Very slowly,' he said, 'back.'

Hope looked at him. 'Why?'

'There's no shadow,' he said. 'That's what was wrong. There's no shadow. That's not him. It's not right.'

'Are you kidding me?'

'Back,' said Perry.

Hope looked at him, examining his eyes. She swore under her breath.

'Back, everyone,' she called slowly. 'Back up.'

Ten minutes later, back at the police car, Hope was making a call to the army. She needed to get the place checked. It was the rest of the day before the army came down and a specialist team went through the building. There were explosives, a tripwire bomb, set for entry into the building.

It took them several hours to defuse it. That evening, the army had searched the building thoroughly, and it was discovered that a small device, which projected the image of a person, was there. It was incredibly modern, and from a distance the hologram was fantastic. But the sun had been shining, and the shadow that a person should have generated was not there.

It was two in the morning when the army was finished, and Hope got back in the car with Perry to return to the office. She turned the key in the ignition and then stopped. Her hands went up to the steering wheel.

'Perry,' she said. Her hands were shaking. 'You just saved my life.'

'Well, yes,' said Perry, 'but I did save my own at the same time.'

Interlude 8

There's a moment when you're at your weakest, when you think you've achieved something. It's a time when you see that something has been resolved and resolved well. And that is the period when you're at your most vulnerable. Because you sigh.

You release the tension You let go and your mind wanders. Your mind thinks about something else. That's the moment that you sigh. That's the moment that you take your eye off the ball. Everything becomes too clear.

You see, the muddied water makes you focus. But when you think it's crystal clear, you're not really bothering to look. Then you realise it wasn't the moment at all; that was just something set up for you—not something that meant it was over.

Chapter 21

Macleod stepped down off the stage. He was at his limit with the press conferences. Almost at a point of sending in Jim, the assistant ACC. He was getting sick of the almost taunts coming from reporters, saying he was behind the curve, asking could *he* cut it anymore.

They were just a distraction. Just vultures who were getting on his nerves when he needed to focus clearly. What didn't help was the pressure from above. Jim was usually sympathetic and knew to leave Macleod alone. But right now, he was behind the curve, being distinctly picky with his questions.

That was because of the pressure Jim was getting from above, getting from everywhere. Macleod had never seen him under such pressure. And that was why Macleod was ignoring some of his phone calls. He didn't wish to talk to him.

Macleod was in his office, staring out of the window, looking at all the press, knowing he should turn away from it. Maybe they'd take photographs, but he had positioned himself just far enough out of reach. Behind him on the desk were the papers. The TV was on in the corner as well. And all the talk was about *The Slaughterhouse* film.

How well it was doing. How the revival had been such

a success. People flocking to it. What was it with people? Didn't they get people were dying out there? What was the fascination with murder?

It was early morning. The day after a late night before. They were still searching, of course. Still looking to see if they could bring Alfonso in, whoever he was. Macleod had counted himself lucky. Perry had saved their lives.

Hope had been keen. Should she have spotted it? It was a tough one. But to go in after him, to assume they'd be safe, was probably unwise. Not that he had to tell her that. The fact her own life was under threat would have been enough.

Macleod had called her and asked her to come and see him. There was a knock at the door. He spun round, gave an 'Enter', and realised it was just his secretary, bringing the coffee in. He turned back, and she knew she didn't need to say anything.

Macleod liked her. She understood pressure; she understood when to tell a joke; understood when to leave him alone. And she could guard him as well. She had told Jim frequently that he wasn't there because he had needed time to think. As she left though, he heard the footsteps of Hope McGrath. He turned to see the tall red-headed inspector, and he was struggling to get a smile.

'I may not look it,' he said, 'but I'm delighted to see you.'

'Too close, Seoras. Too close.'

'You're right there. Good job Perry was with you.'

Hope stood for a moment, reflecting on what had just been said, but then the inspector snapped back in.

'The description that got called in was perfect. I checked at the time, but I thought nothing other than we'd just found him. So, we went for him. The description matched who we were looking for. And it drew us in. First they saw him run, then they saw him in the mill. He must have gone past that area and just cleared out,' said Hope, 'because at some point, they had spotted him, the real him. It was cleverly done.'

'Did you—?'

'Of course we did. We traced the call that gave the information. Pre-pay mobile phone. It's no longer sending out a signal. Although when it did, it was in the Inverness area.'

'They're flocking to see it,' said Macleod. 'If it wasn't for the information we have, I would have said the studio set this up. They're raking the money in.'

'Do you think they've been clever enough,' said Hope, 'to rope somebody in?'

'It's not the studio,' said Macleod. 'It's him. He's the one that's done it. He's come back.'

'Fitz, our machinist. Has Ross had any luck?'

'Everywhere he goes. Every barn, a blank. No.'

Macleod turned again to the window. 'I should go back out there with you. I don't do myself any good staying here.'

'We seem to be following his merry dance,' said Hope. 'Has Clarissa had any luck?'

'She's done all right. We know who it is now, or at least one of them. It'll be Fitz. We've just got to find him.'

'Has she got anywhere with that?'

'Everywhere we go,' said Macleod, 'we can't get a start. We have a funeral; we can't get a description of the only person attending. It's crazy. All we want is a vehicle, a name, an address. Somewhere to start. Because Fitz isn't daft. He's not the one out there. This younger colleague's been the one that's been out there in the main. And if he gets recognised at some point, we're meant to think it's him and not Fitz.'

'Are you all right?' asked Hope. 'Are you okay?'

Macleod was touched by the concern, but he didn't have time for this. 'I'm okay.' said Macleod. 'I'll be all right. You need to focus on the job, not me.'

She stared at him. 'I've never seen you this wound up. I've never seen you—'

'He's come for me. You know that? Come for me and left me no room to wriggle. I'm depending on Clarissa and you. How do we grab these people? This isn't a case of working out who's doing it. I know. I know who's doing it. We just have to find them. And that's going to take all your effort.'

There was a knock on the door. It opened, and his secretary was standing there. 'I'm sorry, Seoras. There's a phone call. It's for Detective Inspector McGrath.'

Macleod waved his hand, and Hope left the room. She was gone for nearly five minutes. When she came back in, her face was drawn; her expression was full of concern.

'What's up?' asked Macleod.

'Two of the searchers have not come back.'

'How long?' asked Macleod.

'Should have been with us an hour ago.'

'And they were together.'

'All searchers are together, in pairs at least. Perry insisted. We always search in teams.'

'Do you know where they've gone?'

'No,' said Hope. 'But I'll find out. Perry'll be on it, anyway, even as we speak.'

'Go,' said Macleod. 'You need to go. Okay?'

Hope turned and left the room, leaving Macleod, pondering this new turn of events. 'Come on, Clarissa,' he said to himself. But in his heart, dreaded hearing more about the two searchers.

* * *

'I've been all over it,' said Perry as Hope arrived.

'Tell me,' said Hope.

'I believe they were looking into a barn. One of the ones that Ross was talking about. They were doing it on the quiet, so they weren't part of the large team. But when they didn't come back . . .'

'Where is it?' asked Hope.

'I'm off there,' said Perry. 'Come with me.'

Hope got into Perry's car and he drove down round a few bends, before there was a barn sitting out near a field. It was certainly big enough for the workshop that Ross had been seeking. Hope watched and there was nothing untoward around the barn. Nobody in sight.

Together, they pulled up, with some police cars following them. Slowly they approached the barn, Hope taking the lead, Perry behind her, scanning every footstep. She looked everywhere, desperate to find something, before she would trigger it. As they were about to enter, from behind them, they heard more cars pulling up. On top of one, Perry saw a satellite dish.

'Stop,' he said to Hope.

'What's happening?'

'Press,' said Perry. 'We've got press. Do you know what that means?'

'Okay,' said Hope, 'we go *very* slowly.'

Perry turned and pointed to the police constables following them, instructing them to make sure they had a wide cordon, and to see if they could turn the press back as best as possible.

'Eyes on me, Perry,' said Hope. 'Eyes on me. Carefully.'

She crept forward towards the barn door. They looked around it and Hope could see footprints. Somebody had entered. She tried to stay clear of them as she slowly opened the door. There was nothing. No indications of any tampering, so delicately she pulled it back.

'Don't open it too far,' said Perry. 'We don't want any of our observers being able to see in.' He was pointing to the press behind him. Hope nodded.

The interior was dark, and Perry appeared on her shoulder, peering in. 'Can you see anything?' she said.

'Let your eyes adjust,' said Perry. She went to step forward, but he grabbed her shoulder. 'I said, "Let your eyes adjust."'

Hope waited. She could feel the tension running through her. Her hands were clammy. She scanned the room.

'I can see something in that corner,' she said to Perry.

'Yes,' he said. 'Let's go round the edge. Don't walk in a direct line.'

Perry took out a pen torch, but rather than shine it across the barn, he turned it on the nearby wall and on the floor. Hope took out her own, sweeping along with him. Hope kept trying to glance over and try to work out what she was seeing in the depths of the barn, but Perry advised against it.

It seemed to take them an age to walk round the side of the barn, along the wall. As they drew closer to the dark of the far wall, Hope stopped, Perry almost bumping in behind her. She lifted her torch beam up, scanning the darkness.

She saw a woman in a police uniform. There was a spike through her leg, pinning her to the wall. 'You see her?' Hope asked Perry.

'Yes, don't rush forward. Take it easy,' said Perry. 'Slowly, very slowly,'

They edged forward another few feet and Hope swung her torch up again on the other wall. She let out a gasp. Perry lifted his beam and his hand shot to Hope's shoulder because he could hear her sudden intake of breath.

'Oh God, Perry,' said Hope, 'he's—'

'He's probably dead,' said Perry slowly. 'Our female colleague, I'm not so sure about. We'll need to keep going slowly and get some medical help to them.'

The image of the dead officer in front of them, the spike through his heart, was a difficult one to see. Together they made their way forward and reached the trapped female officer. As Hope arrived beside her, she touched the woman's shoulder and the woman jerked.

The eyes suddenly opened and the woman tried to speak but only managed a faint gurgle. The wound through her leg was bleeding heavily. Perry looked around.

'Can we get that spike off?' he asked. 'we'll need to do it.'

Together, they pulled at the spike, a device that had been driven up from the floor. Perry held the woman while Hope pushed the mechanism down. Slowly the spike came out of her leg and Perry pulled her backwards, ignoring her distressing moans.

'I've got her,' said Perry.

Hope flashed a torch over at the male officer pinned to the wall.

'He's gone,' said Perry. 'Give me a hand; use our previous footsteps on the way back.'

Slowly, they traced their way back, the woman murmuring in their arms, until eventually they made it through to the front doors of the barn. As they stepped outside holding the woman, Hope could hear the click of cameras. Her eyes squinted in the sunlight, finding it difficult to adjust her sight, but then she saw them all. Seoras had always called them vultures, and she felt he was so right.

She turned and shouted loudly, 'Get me a paramedic, paramedic now!'

Suddenly, several officers ran forward, a first aid kit was brought, and Hope fell to the ground. A sudden release of tension caused her to simply flop but one of the constables went to run inside, and she shouted at him.

'Hold up. Our colleague inside, he's gone. We need to check the building. Wait!'

Chapter 22

'How are you?' asked Clarissa of Patterson. They were finishing off their meal, having heard the distressing news that had come down from Inverness. Two officers down with one dead and one severely injured in the leg. Clarissa looked gaunt. Patterson was clearly in a sour mood.

'He told me he needed me to solve this,' said Clarissa. 'Macleod threw it on to me. He doesn't do that. You know he doesn't do that unless he means it, Pat.'

'So what do you do? What do we do?' asked Patterson. 'How do we solve it?'

'I don't know,' said Clarissa. 'Feel flipping useless. I mean, we've gone down this whole route. We've found out he isn't dead.'

'But we haven't got a line to Fitz.'

'No. But we have got a line to whoever was here. Pats, we know someone was here. We know someone did a mock burial and we've got a falsely filled-in crematorium form.'

'So what do we do with it?' asked Patterson. 'Where can we go? It's a falsely filled-in crematorium form, but it wasn't filled in at a crematorium. Clarissa, it could have been taken from any of them. It's not like we've got a line to Fitz. These forms are easily available. I'm ready for inspiration,' said Patterson. 'I really am. But where do we go?'

'We're out of our jurisdiction really as well. We can't pull in the force from here, there, and everywhere. But we could—'

'Could what?'

'How are your shoes?' asked Clarissa.

'My shoes are fine.'

'They keep your feet comfortable? I mean, can you spend time on them?'

'What are you getting at?' asked Patterson.

'Well, Pats,' said Clarissa, 'We start at the graveyard and we move out in a circle, ever increasing radius. Every B&B, every hotel, every place you can lay your head, to each and every one, we take the description of Alfonso.'

'But there's not much of a description, is there?' said Patterson. 'We've got a rough height on him, but there's not really a—'

'We take what we've got,' said Clarissa. 'It's time to do the spadework.'

As if on cue, the weather outside broke, and rain pelted the window. 'And look,' said Clarissa, 'you'll be thinking you'd want a shawl today. Keep that wind off.'

Patterson shook his head at her. 'Come on, then,' he said. 'At least you have to put the hood up on the car.'

Patterson purchased a map and searched out everywhere you could stay in a radius from the graveyard. He looked up B&Bs, hotels, cottages for hire and they made a plan. The route was marked out. They would go by every single one. Clarissa looked at what was in front of them and didn't know if they would get it all done today. But they would keep going until they did.

The Derbyshire hills didn't always make it easy to know exactly where you were. You were up and down roads, and Clarissa, while she could remember the roads she'd driven upon, was having difficulty relating the map to the road. Patterson, however, was guiding her.

She'd pull up in the car, and together they'd approach the owner of the property. The hotelier, or the B&B owner, responded in the negative each time. By teatime, they'd covered many miles, many, many establishments, and they'd got no positive responses.

'You need to eat,' said Clarissa.

'Chip shop was just back there,' said Patterson. 'Get some chips; we keep going.'

Clarissa nodded. Her shoulders were tired. She was aching but she had to keep going. The trouble was, every time they spoke to someone, the description wasn't much more than a rough height. A vague shape of a man. No idea of the hair colour, no idea of the face.

Did somebody stay here? Yes, they had family. Yes, they had kids. There was no single man. Except one, and he had a full name. He didn't live anywhere near Inverness. And when they phoned up his business, his boss had said he'd been there for the last three weeks, day in, day out. It wasn't him.

They sat and ate their chips together in silence, wondering how long they could go on for during that day.

'Let's go,' Patterson said, and they began again. By the time it got dark, Clarissa was fading badly.

'You keep driving,' he said, 'because I know you won't let me drive this car.'

'Damn right,' said Clarissa.

'Well then,' said Patterson. 'You drive. I'll get out and I'll ask the question.'

'Fair enough,' said Clarissa. She was annoyed with herself. She thought she'd have more stamina than this, but they'd been on quite a tour recently. The night shift when they had popped out to the grave hadn't helped either. Patterson was younger. He could get past things like that. Clarissa was more in need of her sleep than Patterson.

She pulled up outside a small B&B, realising that the time was half past ten.

'We probably should stop. It's the last one, Pats,' she said. 'We can't go annoying people in the middle of the night. Start again first thing in the morning.'

He nodded, and almost robotically got out of the car. He was dragging his feet as he went up the driveway and knocked on the door. She saw the smile. His shoulders suddenly perked up as the door was answered. That was Patterson. Professional, but dedicated too. She was seeing another side of him and she was delighted by it.

Clarissa sat with her head down, looking at the dashboard. She wondered how far it would be to wherever they were going to stay. It was late at night. They had booked nowhere because they didn't know how far they would get. And so, they'd have to just wander into a hotel somewhere. Take what came. She hoped they wouldn't have to drive around several places.

She heard a whistle, like somebody catcalling a woman. She looked around bemused, then realised it was Patterson. Clarissa got out of the car, shawl pulled around her and fought with her own feet to walk over to him. He came towards her.

'I don't want to get your hopes up but—'

'But what?'

'Well, I've got someone that fits the description. I think it might be our man.'

'Why?'

'Come,' said Patterson. Clarissa walked over with him, lifting her heavy feet. The owner of the B&B was standing in a dressing gown.

'This is Mr Jones, and he's kindly answered our call despite being in bed.'

'Forgive our intrusion,' said Clarissa, mustering her best voice. 'I'm Detective Inspector Clarissa Urquhart, Police Scotland. You've met DC Patterson. We're investigating multiple murders and it is very necessary that you talk to us. Can you please repeat what you've told my constable?'

'This boy-o,' said the man, 'he stayed with us a while back.'

Clarissa thought she was in the wrong place, the man's thick Welsh accent ringing in her ears.

'The thing is, this boy, as I was saying, he, well, he fits the description you give, not that it's much of a description. He says to me he was up to do a bit of work. Well, I didn't think he was doing a bit of work, because we have boys that do work, and these lads, they don't come up like this boy-o. They come up with their vans, or they've got their laptops and things with them. This guy, next to nothing. I mean it, next to nothing. The other thing was that he had something in the back of the car he didn't want me to see. I know that, because I was eyeing the car up, and it was nice. Fiesta.'

'You didn't get a reg, did you?'

'No, we don't ask for reg here. We're not like the hotels where you park your car.'

And that's why he would use you, thought Clarissa. 'I take it you got a name from him?'

'I did. And this is what got me, because he said to me first of all, his name was Darren.'

'Oh, okay.'

'He gave me a surname. I can't remember which one he gave me. But when it came to paying, he handed me these Scottish notes. Well, we don't take Scottish notes here. The banks don't like them. So I said to him, I need something else.'

Something inside Clarissa wanted to grab the man and throttle him. Not take Scottish notes. But there was something more important here, so she let him continue.

'I've had people walk off on me. People say I'm not staying because you don't take our money.'

Quite right, thought Clarissa.

'But this guy, he's adamant, he has to stay here. "Why? There're other B&Bs," I said to him. "Further down the road; they'd take your money," I says. I said, "You know, we'd take a card and that." But he didn't want to use a card, right? Said to me he didn't want it on the card. I didn't ask why. I mean, I'm quite happy with cash, too. Doesn't bother me, but I'm not taking the Scottish notes. Take them to the bank and they complain to you. And then he started all this legal tender argument. Well, it's not legal tender, is it?'

'I don't really want to get into the issue of legal tender or not, sir,' said Clarissa, 'just any more information would be useful.'

'Well, he eventually paid by card and stayed here.'

'He paid by card?' blurted Clarissa.

'Yes, he paid by card. Well, sort of. I said to him what he could do with the card, because I would not let him stay without paying up front. Well, he wasn't happy to put it in the machine. He said he'd just give me the details, give me the number and that. I said, well, that's no good to me.

'I said to him, "Look, I've got one of those old machines. The ones where you just stick the card in and you pull the thing across and it prints it out on the paper, you know. Like that tracing stuff." So eventually he agreed to that. But he said I had to rip it up when he gave me the cash.

'Well, I'm not daft. Not happy about this. So, the next day when he comes with English money, and he gives me it, the boy-o says give me the card receipt. So I did. I gave him the top copy and ripped it up right there in front of him. He obviously wasn't used to that stuff, though, because of course, there's three copies. He got two of them ripped up but I kept the other one.

'Don't know why. I just wasn't happy. I thought of it as collateral, in case something happened to the room. Anyway, I filed it away, so it's in here.'

'Can you get me it, please?' asked Clarissa. The man disappeared inside the house. Clarissa looked at Patterson. 'We got it, Pats. We got our link.' Patterson was smiling.

'Let's hope so,' he said. 'Let's hope so.'

The man came back out in his dressing gown, holding a slip of paper. Clarissa looked at it. The detail was worn, but it was legible. 'Can I just step inside a moment?' she asked. 'I want to take a photograph of this. Then I'm going to have to put it in an evidence bag. Take it from you, if that's okay, sir. I'll write you a receipt for it. I'll say we've got it. It's not a problem.'

'It's no use to me now anyway,' he said. 'I mean, he didn't break anything. Disappeared off on his way. That's the name on the card, though, and it's different to the one he gave you.'

'It is.'

'He tried to say it was his brother-in-law's card or something. The only thing he had with him, making up some cock-and-bull story.'

Clarissa took out her phone, and took a photograph of the sheet of paper. She then produced a little small evidence bag, dropping the sheet into it and sealing it.

'You know what?' said Clarissa. 'I'm very sorry we inconvenienced you, but you may have just turned the tide on this one. Thank you very much, sir.' She put her hand out and shook it.

'Well, you're looking a lot happier than when you arrived. There's lovely,' he said. 'I hope you get the boy-o. All the best, eh?'

'All the best,' said Clarissa. Patterson was walking back to the car. He was about to get in the passenger side when he felt Clarissa tap him on the shoulder. He turned round, and she flung her arms around him.

'Nice one,' she said. 'Nice one, Pats.'

He stood there, being embraced like he never knew what a hug was before. She stepped back, smiling at him.

'We did it,' she said. 'We did it. You did it. You kept going. I was over.'

'Do you not think you should be telling Macleod about this one?' he said. He was so deadpan. And if he hadn't of just let his smile appear at the edge of his mouth, she would have thought he wasn't joking.

'You phone him,' said Clarissa. 'You deserve it.'

'No, no. It's the arts team,' said Patterson. 'We did it. You're the boss, so you tell him. He put the pressure on you, not on me. And you got him. You got it for him.'

Clarissa picked up her phone and called Macleod direct on his mobile.

'What is it?' he said,

'Seoras, we've done it. I've got your link. I've got your sodding link.'

She told him the story and then she messaged him the image of the evidence. Clarissa followed that up by messaging it to Hope and to Ross as well, just in case Macleod screwed up passing the image on.

'You still on the other end of the phone?' There was silence. 'Don't I get anything for that? Don't I get a well done?'

'Well done,' he said, 'it's been a rough day. You probably deserve more than that but that's what you're getting. Get yourself back up here.'

The call was closed down, and Clarissa turned to Patterson in the car.

'I take it he's happy,' said Patterson.

'Were you expecting to get to bed?' she said.

'Kind of,' said Patterson. 'I think we've done our bit today. I mean, there's not much else for us to do around here, is there?'

'I want to drive up tonight.'

'Why,' asked Patterson, 'if you don't mind me asking,'

'He's not right,' she said. 'Macleod isn't himself.'

'You've had a long day,' said Patterson, 'and you're seriously telling me you want to drive all the way up tonight. That's not safe; that's not,'

'You can drive half of it,' she said.

'What?' said Patterson. 'I get to drive half of it?'

'You heard me,' she said. 'Get to sleep. I'll drive the first couple of hours, then you can take over.'

'You're going to let me drive your car?'

'Yes,' said Clarissa. 'Now get to sleep. You'll need it for when you take over.'

'He's really not right, is he?' said Patterson. Clarissa shook her head. He had got her really worried now.

Chapter 23

There was certainly a determination in those at the station but the death of their colleague meant everything was done in a subdued fashion. Macleod stared out of his window, knowing that they had to keep working, to keep going, to find who was doing this. Whenever you lost one of your own, it sometimes brought it home how dangerous the profession was. It wasn't unheard of for an officer to die, but thankfully, at least here in Scotland, it was rare.

He had just finished watching it again. Macleod couldn't fathom why anyone would want to watch *The Slaughterhouse*. Why did people want to see horror? What was it that made them so fascinated by it?

For Macleod, being a police officer, wasn't because of any fascination with the evil and darkness that he saw during the job. Instead, his was a compulsion that wrongs had to be put right. It was a just cause. Yes, he would be lying if he didn't say he was intrigued and excited by working out the puzzles, by examining the people. Well, that was certainly one of the more stimulating aspects of the job. Still, there was a part of him that would rather the job didn't exist, that there was no need for it.

There came a knock at the door and Macleod told the new arrival to come in. Hope stepped through and she looked tired to Macleod. Her ponytail wasn't neatly done, and she pulled it out, adjusting her hair before fixing it up again. She didn't do that in front of Seoras. She usually made herself presentable before she went anywhere, especially coming up to the more senior floor.

'You okay?' she asked.

'As well as can be expected,' said Macleod. 'Tragic. Just tragic. Maybe we should have seen it coming.'

'Thankfully, one of them survived.'

'She had to watch him die, though,' said Macleod. 'It's horrific. But we'll get him.'

'He's played it straight though all along,' said Hope.

'What do you mean by that?'

'He's followed the film. He's done what the film says he will do. That means there's one death left. It's a senior investigator. It's this senior investigator.' She pointed at Macleod.

'I am aware of that,' said Macleod.

'I take it Jane's not?'

Macleod thought of his partner sitting at home, and there was no way he would burden her with that.

'You could always just depart, go on a three-week holiday.'

'And what?' said Macleod. 'You step up and become that senior investigator? This is my case. It was given to me.'

'You said I was capable of it. You said—'

'I still believe that,' said Macleod, 'but it was given to me. When you're given a job, you carry it out. You get it done,'

'Have you seen the papers? Jane's going to see the papers soon.'

'Jane doesn't read the papers,' said Macleod. 'I try to stay away from them as best I can. Papers are just, well, you know.'

'What is it with you?' spat Hope. 'This isn't you. We've just had a colleague die. You would slam the desk. You would race to get this person.'

'Sometimes you have to look at the bigger picture,' said Macleod.

'What bigger picture?' asked Hope. 'What? This guy wants to put you in a grave. He's practically told you how he's going to do it as well.'

Macleod thought back to the film. There was a graphic moment at the end, where the senior investigator lost his head. Macleod had seen it several times and with the implication that it would be him. He turned away from Hope.

'We've all got to face things,' he said. 'This is mine to face.'

'It's not a game,' said Hope. 'This is your life we're talking about!'

'Whoever's life,' said Macleod. 'Whoever stands in this role, it's their life at risk. Of course it is. And it is a game.'

Hope looked at him, bemused. 'When did you ever think that? When did you ever—'

'The big picture,' Macleod said suddenly. 'The big picture, Hope. Look at the big picture.' He sighed and walked round to the back of his desk and sat down. He looked at some paperwork in front of him, picked up a pen and signed some off.

'I'll keep you updated,' said Macleod. 'I promise. Perry did well. So did you. It's never nice finding someone like that. But you got in safely and got out. One of our colleagues is alive because you did that.'

'It's what we do,' said Hope. 'And we're going to catch this bastard.'

'Bastards,' said Macleod. 'It's not one.'

Hope stared at him. He wasn't particularly animated. But he was certainly deep in thought. She left the room and Macleod almost breathed a sigh of relief. It was hard with people around him at the moment. He needed to think. He needed to match this person. But how? How did he do that? Maybe they could get him, get him before it all played out.

It was later that morning when there was a knock on the door. Ross marched into the room, having waited several seconds without getting a reply.

'Sorry to barge in on you, sir,' said Ross. 'I think, well, I think I've got it.'

'Got what?' asked Macleod.

'The address for the credit card.'

'Good. Who else knows?'

'No one, I came straight to you.'

'Any of the constables know?'

'No. I have told no one.'

'Good. Don't let it go outside of our group. Me, Perry, Hope, Clarissa, Patterson, Susan, no one else. We keep it tight.'

'Why?'

'We need to catch them both,' said Macleod. 'If it gets out that we're on to them, one of them won't come. We need them both.'

'So, what do I do instead?' asked Ross.

'Perry. Get Perry to observe the building. Tell Hope. Perry will see anyone coming in who's different. Will understand who they are.'

Ross nodded. 'Shouldn't we have a strike team or someone on duty ready to leap into action with us? I don't think we should take these people down ourselves.'

'Won't come to that,' said Macleod.

'Okay.'

Ross left the room somewhat bemused but Macleod continued to sit at his desk. It was ten minutes later when he heard the thud coming up the stairs. The door wasn't knocked, simply flung open, and then slammed closed, almost hitting Patterson in the face.

'Hello,' said Macleod.

'Patterson, stay out there,' said Clarissa. She looked awful.

'I haven't driven half the night to have you play games.'

'Excuse me,' said Macleod. 'I think you need to know your place here. This is my call.'

'I have waded in for you. Waded in. I have pulled you out of the fire. And I am not having you voluntarily offer yourself up out of some sort of idea that it's a righteous thing to do.'

'There's no righteousness in it,' said Macleod.

'I know you. I know you, Seoras Macleod. What are you doing? Hope says you're barely talking to her about this. Hope says—'

'If Hope's got a problem, she can come see me,' said Macleod.

'Seoras, damn it!' said Clarissa. 'This is your life we're talking about. You! This isn't just anyone.'

'Are you telling me we've just lost someone, and that didn't matter?'

'That's not fair. That is completely unfair. Dammit, I got you your evidence. I got you your trace. Keep out of it. Let us go find them.'

'I am going to find them. Perry's on the case. He'll find them. But we might not have time for that.'

'You should stay in. Stay clear. You know how it ends. You've seen the film.'

'I've seen the film over ten times now,' said Macleod, 'mostly through the quiet hours. What makes people watch stuff like this?' said Macleod quietly.

'What? I'm not going to give you some sort of Barry Norman exposition,' said Clarissa. 'At the end of the day, we're talking about you, and I'm not going to lose you. I've gone through enough with you. I have pulled you away from the jaws of death.'

'And I thank you, but remember I'm the DCI. I call the shots. I'll tell you how to play it.'

'I never thought I'd say this to you,' said Clarissa, 'but you're being reckless. Albeit you're being reckless with your own life, you're still being reckless and fatalistic. You don't have to play this scene out. You don't have to.'

'That's where you're wrong,' said Macleod. 'I do have to play it out.'

'Why?'

'You'll see,' he said.

'What's that meant to mean? Why are you being cryptic?'

'Well done down there,' said Macleod suddenly. 'Well done. Solid, old-fashioned bit of police work. Digging your way in. I'm really pleased with you,' said Macleod. 'You've done a—'

'Don't tell me I've done a fantastic job. Bloody well, answer me properly.'

'Go see if Hope needs some help,' said Macleod.

'Is that it? Suddenly dismissed.'

'You got me what I needed from the art world. It's no longer part of the investigation. I know what's coming. I know what I have to do.'

'Seoras!'

'That's it,' he said. 'You can go. And if Hope hasn't got something for you right now, get some sleep.'

'Do you realise,' she said, 'I let Patterson drive half of the way up.'

Macleod looked up for a moment before putting his head back down. 'He drives very well, I'm sure.'

'I'm going to come back and knock some sense into you,' said Clarissa. She turned, stormed off to the door, pulled it open and nearly crashed into Patterson, who was still standing there.

'Out of the way,' said Clarissa. She marched past Patterson. He stepped briefly inside of the office, staring over at Macleod.

'Shall I close the door for you, sir?'

'Absolutely.'

Macleod stood up, turned and looked out the window. Press. Vultures. This was all being played out in front of the press. This was an ego trip. Fitz's ego trip, he thought. I have to bait him. I have to, somehow, bring him in. How do we do it? How do I do it?

Macleod stared down, looking at the press. *Vultures indeed, but if you're going to show off to the press, it's because you need to be there. He'll want his machines in the spotlight. And the last one would be quite a machine. Like the blade that took the officer's head in the film.* There was a shiver running down Macleod's back. He had to go with this. He had to do it.

Macleod turned back to his desk, sat down and signed a few more bits of paperwork. Then he stopped. There was a cold cup of coffee off to the far side of the desk and he picked it up and drank a sip. Yeah, it was cold, but it still tasted all right. And he also had something in his head now. An option. Would it work? He didn't know, but it would be better than standing around waiting for the inevitable.

Once again, Macleod stood up, went to the window, but took his phone with him. He dialled a number.

'Hello, I'm looking for something. I wonder if you could help me.'

Interlude 9

There comes a time in the film when everything must be tied together. But you have to make sure that everyone's there. We'll wait on Macleod. We'll pull him in. He'll have to come. He'll have to finish it.

He'll take it hard. They take it hard when they lose one of their own. It's the way he is. Understand the man. Understand how to pull the strings. He'll die. But he'll die being the thorough, brave, and honest man that he is. That's how we shot the film the first time round. That's why it works and why there's the shock.

They've seen Macleod be successful so often, it wouldn't be the same with somebody else. He's the one who's coped; he's the one that's managed it all. Macleod is the one who's survived, and he even survived a cult.

That's the crux of it. When somebody's been built up so high and they're seen as being so strong, when you pull that away from them—when you suddenly click your fingers and end it—that's when they become your biggest shock. And it's what people remember.

When the viewer walked away from the last scene, the first time the film was shown, that's what they remembered. And they'll remember Macleod. He should thank me, really. He's going to be the victim of one of my best machines. Yes, he really should thank me for his immortalisation.

His death will be poetic. It'll be sudden and violent but poetic. A man going out the way he should. Doing his job and doing it well. And putting his safety behind that of the others. It's inevitable. In this real life, it's inevitable, just like the film. It's all swum along beautifully so far; it won't stop.

Chapter 24

There was a knock at Macleod's door. He asked for the caller to come in, and his secretary appeared. She advised him that Miss Nakamura would like him to attend a meeting down in Hope's office, saying there was fresh evidence. Macleod nodded, stood up, and trudged down to the office he'd called home for so long.

Inside, he could see the team assembled: Perry, Susan Cunningham, Ross, Clarissa, Patterson, and, of course, Hope. She was eyeing him as he walked in, and there was a quietness in the room.

'So,' said Macleod, 'Jona's called this meeting; therefore, I think Jona should start. What have you got for us?'

'Well,' said Jona, 'it comes from our unfortunate colleague. They must have been close when it happened, for there was a note left inside his clothing.'

'What?' said Macleod.

'A piece of paper. Torn paper inside the clothing of our dead officer. It isn't his handwriting. It belongs to our foe. No fingerprints I can find, but there is an address on it.'

'That's a trap,' said Clarissa, but Macleod put his hand up.

'We're sure it's not our officer's handwriting.'

'No. It's definitely someone else,' said Jona.

'Anything else?'

'No. Just the handwriting.'

'I take it you've done all the other analyses.'

'Of course, there's nothing. I can't work anything more out from it. Sorry.'

Macleod nodded and stood up. He walked around the table while being watched by the others.

'This is a trap,' said Clarissa. 'This is him pulling you in.'

'Have we got any further with the machines?' Macleod asked. 'Susan?'

'No. We're still where we were. We haven't been able to trace any of the parts. They've all been bought from general stores, anywhere that you can pay with cash. We can't tie it down to one area, one place. They could have bought them from anywhere. Anything that's unique is machined. So, we're looking at a warehouse.'

'We don't want to be looking at any more warehouses after what happened,' said Macleod.

'But you can't go through with this. This is him completing his work,' said Hope. 'It's too risky. You know what will happen. You've seen what happens in the film.'

'This is not a film. And even if it is, this is how we get him,' said Macleod. 'This is—'

'This is how he gets you,' said Clarissa. 'He will put you in the same situation. Better you stay outside. Better you don't do any of this.'

'And if I don't, he'll disappear. He'll run. He'll play it out the way he wants it to play out, and we'll just end up with another dead body. One of our own, with another note. And—'

'I know I haven't been on the entire case. Looking at it from the point of view of the killer,' said Jona, 'Seoras is right. It sounds to me like this guy will not back away unless he gets his proper finale. He's got time, after all.'

'Doesn't matter, we don't give him that finale,' said Hope. 'It's too risky. Seoras should stay here. Put him in a van outside!'

'Excuse me, put him in a van outside?' said Macleod. 'I'm the DCI here, and the DCI will take charge and run it. I don't suppose that this address corresponds to the address we're watching at the moment.'

'I'm unaware of that address,' said Jona, and she put the piece of paper on the table, wrapped in its evidence bag. Macleod leaned over and looked at it.

'Two addresses then.' He walked away to the window, staring out, looking down at a familiar but comforting area.

'I'm with Clarissa on this one,' said Patterson. 'I think you're putting yourself in too much danger. With respect, sir.'

'I'm with him on that,' said Ross. 'Patterson's right, sir.'

'What do you think, Perry?' asked Hope.

Perry was silent. Susan said, 'Sir, seems an awful risk, especially while you've got one address. We could always just not go to this one, make out it was lost, and then—'

'And then he finds another way to deliver it. And he may like to deliver that one with a body, because he will think one body isn't enough for Macleod to come, and he'll kill again until I come. No, I need to end this now.'

'No, you don't,' said Clarissa, 'you don't. Have one of us pick him up. Don't follow the script. Don't run in.'

'It's all been about the script. It's all been about his machines,' said Macleod. 'He didn't want to be famous. He wants his machine, the one that took down Macleod, to be famous. That's why it's me. You all get that, don't you? Perry?'

'I do,' said Perry, 'and I think you're right with that. You're the one he wants. If you hand it all over to me, we won't see the machine, and he'll make you come on another day. Goad you into it, I would reckon.'

'This is the opportunity to end it,' said Macleod, 'before anybody else gets hurt. He hasn't given us that option yet. This is the option. This is the one we take.'

'Let me get Jim down. Discuss it with Jim. You're putting a—'

'Hope, this is my pay grade,' said Macleod. 'This is what I'm paid to do, and I will finish it.'

'And what if he puts it in front of you? Shows you the exact same thing we have in the film. Will you follow it?,' asked Clarissa. 'Will you go and do what happened in the film?'

'The policeman in the film goes down on his hands and knees inside one of the machines,' said Hope. 'Because there's something there. He'll do that, put something there. He'll make you think that—'

'I know,' said Macleod. 'I'm well aware of that. We go. I have to pick something up first though. Once I've done that, we'll go. He'll be there to gloat. So we'll pick him up there, you understand? Perry, I want you at the other address, and I want it raided as soon as we give the word. But while we're at the address on the piece of paper, you watch the one we got from the credit card.'

'I'm coming with you,' said Hope. 'I'll be right by your side. I'll be watching you. I'm your DI, I'm your number two!'

'And I'm your number three,' said Clarissa. 'I'm coming, too. I can't have you doing something stupid. In fact, we should take a whole—'

'No,' said Macleod. 'In the film, there's only a couple of

officers who go. Any more will scare him off. He won't like it. The more I scare him off, the more likely he might do something to Jane, or move outside the police force. We've been fortunate so far.'

'Fortunate. In what way?' asked Clarissa.

'He could have gone a lot more brutal. We're going to end it,' said Macleod; 'this is how we end it. And you Ross,' said Macleod, 'make sure you get ready to search the man's accounts when I arrest him.'

'Yes sir, of course.'

'Susan, be ready with our machinist. We may need someone to come in and make things safe.'

She nodded. 'Right,' said Macleod. 'So we're all sorted. I'll be back in an hour. Be ready to go.'

Macleod turned and left the room, which wasn't normal form. He usually would wait for the others to leave, but he thought today they wouldn't go quickly. He needed no more debate. His mind was made up. He knew what was going to happen. He knew what he was going to do. That was it. There was no more thinking to be done.

Macleod stomped up the stairs into his office, sat down, and signed a few more bits of paper before getting back up and picking up his coat from the coat hanger. He put it on, stepped outside, and told the secretary he'd be about forty minutes.

He made his way down to his car. Inside, he turned on the ignition, and then stopped. His hands were trembling on the wheel.

'Come on, Seoras,' he said; 'you can do this.' He put the foot down on the accelerator, reversed out, and then spun the large car out towards the main road.

Chapter 25

Macleod sat in the front seat as Hope drove with Clarissa in the rear. She had offered to take her little sports car round, but Macleod had a bit of luggage with him, a bag that the two women kept staring at.

'Just what is it you've brought with you?' asked Hope.

'It's my box of tricks,' said Macleod. 'You're all worried I'm going to die. This is what's going to keep me alive.'

'What will keep you alive' said Clarissa, 'is sending the army in here first, or a strike team, or something of that nature. Just the three of us?'

'Just the three of us,' said Macleod. 'You can't do it with a cast of thousands in a film, can you? With three people, the emotions are more intense. They're not dispersed amongst everyone. I'm starting to understand this film lark,' said Macleod.

'I'm not sure you do,' said Clarissa. 'I'm not convinced you understand this guy.'

'Better than you think,' said Macleod. But his tone was even if slightly sombre.

They arrived in front of a house that looked much like any other. It was detached, but it wasn't overly large. Through the front living room window, Macleod could see a bare room. Even from the road where the car was parked, it was obvious. There was a short wall around the garden, but as Macleod stepped out of the car to approach, the place almost looked banal.

He could have seen a family living here, except there was nothing to show someone lived here. There were no curtains up for a start. He wondered how it was possible. Was this the right place? After all, if there were no curtains, people could watch a machinist build. For there would be a machine, wouldn't there?

Macleod went to step onto the driveway, but Hope grabbed him. 'No, Seoras. Easy, like myself and Perry did. One bit at a time. One—'

'You forget, don't you?' said Macleod. 'It's not what happened in the film. He didn't shoot him out in the open. He didn't blow him away. The senior investigator lost his head. Lost his head at the end of a tunnel.'

'But there's no tunnel. It makes little sense,' said Clarissa. 'It really doesn't make any sense.'

Macleod nodded, but continued forward to the front door. He put his hand up to rap it, but as his fist struck the door, the door swung open. Macleod stared at the view in front of him. Normally, this would have been a hallway, stairs to the upper floors on the right-hand side. But the hallway had been sectioned, so that there was a top half to it and a lower half.

The top half was cut off by a mesh screen. Macleod could see through the mesh and could see that a flat section at about waist height had been placed in the hallway. It looked fairly solid, and it meant that you could either crawl down and along what was effectively a small corridor or tunnel to the far end.

The other option was to take this mesh off and walk on top. Macleod stood for a moment looking at the tunnel.

'I'm not sure the top half's going to be a good idea,' said Hope to Macleod. Hope pointed to some wires that were attached to the mesh. 'Could be you get a shock or something stronger than that.'

'We could go left into the sitting room,' said Hope. There was a doorway just before the tunnel started.

Macleod reached over, went to turn the knob, but Clarissa shouted at him to stop.

'Look,' she said. 'Hope said about the mesh, but that wire runs to the door as well.'

More mesh covered the stairs option.

'Clearly I'm meant to go down this tunnel,' said Macleod. 'I mean, I've seen the film. I shall go down it and see what's at the far end.'

'No, you won't,' said Clarissa. 'I'll do it.'

'And what if you meet your demise? He'll still come for the rest of us. He wants me, needs me to finish. Better that he finish with me than take one of you to come back at me again.'

'Don't speak like that,' said Clarissa. 'What is it with you? This is not like you. You don't talk like that. You don't.'

'Trust me,' said Macleod. 'You need to trust me. This is the ending. This is where it all happens. We've been caught in a film.' He gave a wry smile. 'I wonder does he know how much I hate the media, the spotlight? I wonder does he knows how thorough I am. But above all, I wonder does he know how I like the challenge. Does he know Macleod?'

'What do you mean?' asked Clarissa.

'Me?' said Macleod. 'How much does he know me?'

He bent down onto his knees, and with the bag he was

carrying in front of him, he began to make his way down through the tunnel. Occasionally, his head lifted and caught the top of it, for it was low. He wasn't sure his knees or his joints would get him that far.

'I'm okay,' he said, crawling down.

'Not a good idea, Seoras,' said Hope.

'I'm fine. Is there anyone at the far end? Can you see anything down there?'

'Nothing. Absolutely nothing,' said Hope.

'Me neither, but we can't get too close to this mesh. I can't see properly,' said Clarissa. 'Remember in the film, it's when he stands up, it's when he gets to the end of the tunnel and stands up, then he's attacked, and he loses his head,' said Clarissa. 'Stay low. Whatever you do, Seoras, stay low.'

'I don't intend to lose my head,' said Macleod. 'I really don't.'

He continued down along the tunnel, sweat beginning to run across his face. Soon he was close to the end of the hallway, the converted tunnel, but in front of him was a solid piece of metal. There was a gap above him now, and he could stand up if he wanted to. In fact, if he wanted to get into the kitchen beyond, he'd have to step up and over the metal.

'What's happening?' asked Hope.

'Blocked off at the lower level. I'll have to get up and go over it.'

'No,' said Hope. 'Don't. Come back. It's when he stands up that it all goes wrong.'

'Nothing here,' said Macleod. 'I can see absolutely nothing.'

'But he's the master of these traps,' said Clarissa. 'Susan didn't see hers coming. That's the point. Our two officers. One's dead because they didn't see their trap coming. This is . . . this is . . . Just don't,' said Clarissa.

'It'll be fine,' said Macleod. 'It'll be fine.'

* * *

Hope stared down the tunnel. She was down low, looking at Macleod. He had his back to her and he'd said that there wouldn't be a problem. *There would be a problem*, she thought. *Of course there would be a problem.* She glanced across at Clarissa. Her eyes were as wide as the moon, and she was almost pale.

'You need to stop him.'

'He's too far down now,' said Hope. 'He'll not be stopped.'

'I'm just going to clamber up and over. It's perfectly safe. There's nothing here.'

Hope stood up, looking down over the top of the tunnel to the far end. She saw Macleod's head begin to rise up. Then she saw his ears. And then she heard the swish. She watched in horror as his head lifted, cut by an enormous blade that swept in from the wall. The head took off, landing in the kitchen. She dropped, almost in disbelief, to look down the tunnel. Macleod's body, his feet towards her, was lying flat.

Clarissa screamed. Hope found the bile flying up in her throat. She went to put a hand to her mouth, when the door beside her suddenly opened, and someone jumped on her. There was something hitting her then, striking her in the back of the head. She fell down.

'Oh, you bloody don't,' shouted Clarissa.

Hope tried to roll out of the way, half into the tunnel, and she saw Clarissa's feet stepping forward. There was a cry from a man, and then Clarissa shouted too. Hope was groggy, extremely groggy, and she tried to roll back out of the tunnel. Clarissa had somehow pushed the man backwards, maintaining his cudgel up above her. She didn't allow it to be struck down. Hope kicked out at the man's knees.

He dropped slightly, and as she tried to get to her feet in some woozy fashion, she saw Clarissa drive her shoulder into the man. He dropped, and Clarissa snatched the cudgel off of him. She hit him once across the head, and then she hit him again. Then there was a third attack.

Hope was reeling in disbelief. She looked back down the top of the tunnel, and there was nothing. Absolutely nothing. She fell onto her backside, her head spinning, eyes swimming, tears forming. It didn't look like she was going to stop. She was shouting at the man. Swearing. Calling him everything. Telling him he was a goner. Telling him he was scum. Clarissa was almost wild with rage.

As Hope sat with her back on the wall, unable to stand, she saw a figure emerge from the tunnel. It stood upright, and a loud and commanding voice said. 'Detective Inspector Urquhart. Put that down and leave him alone. And would you arrest him properly.'

Hope looked up. He was there, in his coat, his tie done up properly, his hair was barely out of place. There was no blood, there was nothing, his neck intact. Macleod turned round and smiled at Hope.

'Got him,' he said. 'Got him.' He was pulling out his mobile, and he rang a number. As he did so, Clarissa looked at him in total shock. Hope sat with her mouth hanging open. Their attacker, an older man, lay mumbling, heavily battered. Macleod, happy that the call had gone through, said just two words, 'Perry, go.'

Hope saw a hand being offered to her, and she took

Macleod's hand and stood up. He looked over at the man on the floor.

'That,' he said, 'I believe is Fitz. I'm not feeling the best, so if you don't mind, I'll go sit in the car. If you would just kindly arrest him and bring him along, we'll get the team down here and talk about it at the station. Well done, everyone.'

Macleod walked out through the front door. Hope didn't know what to make of it. Was she dreaming? Part of her wanted to shout for joy, but another part was ready to swing for him.

Chapter 26

It had been a gruelling afternoon, and Macleod emerged from the interview room with Hope. In the next room, he could see Perry sitting with Clarissa, talking to Alfonso. Perry had arrested him straight away, for the man had been at the house with the credit card address.

Stephen Fitz had been easy to interview, for the man talked candidly and excitedly about everything he had done. Macleod had suspected this—had thought that the man was an exhibitionist of sorts. The reasons he was this way were troubling Macleod.

Having seen Perry winding up his interview, Macleod asked the officer standing outside the interview room to send Perry and Clarissa upstairs to the office. He chose to go to Hope's, and the team in the main office were working away, pulling together the last connections.

There was still a sombre mood in the station. As he walked along, making his way up the stairs to the office, several officers stopped him and simply shook his hand. He'd got the man who'd killed their colleague. They weren't in a mood to rejoice, but they were glad he had done it.

Macleod walked to the coffee machine, telling Hope to go

inside and he'd bring the cups through. He was almost back to being himself, or so he told himself. At least, that's the way he wanted to be. He told Jane he'd be home that night, but that he had a lot of paperwork to do.

Clarissa ignored Macleod making the coffee and went straight into the office beside Hope. Perry walked over to take over from Macleod but he waved him away and told him to wait here in the inner office. As he went to, Macleod told him to pick Ross up on the way.

Jona was busy, still out at the house, as was Susan Cunningham, accompanying her machine expert from the college. Jona would need help to make sure that things were safe. Macleod thought they would be, but you had to be certain, because these machines were deadly.

Macleod wandered in with the coffees on a tray, placed the tray on Hope's main desk, and then lifted the coffees across, placing them in front of everyone. Following that, he sat down.

'Stephen Fitz,' said Macleod, 'is a deeply disturbed genius. I don't know if it's from drugs or from abuse of some other sort, but what I can say is, he was the planner behind all of this. He's the genius, and he's just sat and calmly told us all about it. I would be wrong to say that he was modest about it. He was bragging.'

Hope nodded. 'And we'll get a conviction because we're going to have a confession. And it's going to check out all along the line.'

'That's the strange thing,' said Perry. 'Alfonso was the same. He's like a worshipper of Fitz's abilities. He didn't stop talking about him the whole time, telling us how he was taking Alfonso through everything, helping him, guiding him. Alfonso thought it was just great to be part of it. And he was going to get paid handsomely. Though he wouldn't say by who.'

'I can help with that,' said Ross. 'As soon as Perry arrested Alfonso, I got into his accounts. It's quite clear he's getting paid by, I believe, someone from the new studio. Consulting fees, it's called. Fitz, I think, is getting the same. The trouble is that the money's gone round the houses. It might not be the studio as a whole, it might be an executive. In time,' said Ross, 'we'll make the connection. It'll be a fight but we should get someone for it.'

'You did well, everyone,' said Macleod. 'You did really well. We were chasing ghosts. Chasing people from the past that were dead. And we lost people on the way.'

'Two days' time,' said Hope, 'in case you don't know.'

'Well done. I've not lost many in the line of duty, but this one, well, I don't want to say any more. I'll say something at the funeral,' explained Macleod, 'because I've been invited to. Until then, we have to tidy everything up. Dot the I's, cross the T's, and then off to the funeral. When the paperwork's done, we'll have a party. We need to let this out, need to let it go. We need to have something that marks the end.'

Ross stood up and walked around to Macleod, holding out a hand.

'Well done,' he said, 'I really struggled with this. He was good. He was too good; understood how to keep out of everything.'

'He did,' said Macleod. 'Alfonso blew it for him, really, but Clarissa got the breakthrough. Good old-fashioned police work, not something like me and Perry are used to,' said Macleod. 'I said to them, Hope should have run this investigation, because that's where it was found.'

Ross nodded, then departed, and the rest of the team stood

up. Perry shook hands with Macleod, exited the room, leaving the two women with him.

'You can stand there, and you can tell them all this platitude,' said Clarissa, 'but you will not brush me off like that. I thought you were dead. Didn't you get me the first time I told you? I got out of the murder team because I wanted no more trauma. I didn't want to see people die.'

'You didn't. Hope saw the officer.'

'I saw you die,' said Clarissa. 'I would have beaten him to death.'

'Which is why I got back up that tunnel quickly,' said Macleod. 'I had to do it. I had to pull the killer out. There was no other way of getting him. We would have got Alfonso. But you had to be in the dark. Thank you for your efforts,' said Macleod. 'You busted it open. You got us Alfonso. You gave me the opportunity.'

'Don't,' she said. 'Just don't. Never play me like that again. You got something up your sleeve? You tell me what it is. Never, ever, play me like that. I could have killed that man. In fact, I think part of me still could.'

Clarissa turned, throwing her shawl around her shoulder, and marched out of the door, slamming it behind her.

'You deserve that,' said Hope. Macleod nodded, turned and walked behind her desk to stand, looking out at the view he loved so much.

'Would you and the window like some time alone?' asked Hope.

Macleod chortled. But his hands were shaking.

'You all right?' said Hope.

Macleod shook his head. 'When you were down there with him, interviewing him, did you feel it? Did you really feel it?'

'What do you mean?' asked Hope.

'Fitz got the money. But he would have done it without it. He just wanted to see his machines work, wanted to put himself up above everyone else. He wanted to take me out, to put himself on a pedestal up above me. To put himself as the person. Up above all. Do you understand? Do you understand he would kill people, and he did kill people, to lift himself up?'

'Where are you coming from?'

'You're not from my background, Hope. So, I understand that you're not seeing it. That was the devil's sin. He wanted himself up above everybody else, and he was prepared to take everybody else down to do it. That's what Fitz did.

'I have seen many motives for murder. I have seen people betrayed, people in love, people do it for money, and I have seen people do it because their child is at risk. Because they can't live without someone. I've seen them do it for anger, do it for greed. But this was a joy in killing. This was something that said, "I can destroy you to lift me up." That's evil, Hope. In my book, that's true evil.'

He turned back and his hands were still shaking. He stared out of the window where the rain had just started.

'In some ways, Hope, he won.'

'I don't see that,' said Hope. 'You got him, you won.'

'No, I didn't. I merely caught him. The press are all over this; the film is everywhere. What have we done other than play our part? I saved my own neck, and don't get me wrong, Hope; I'm glad I did it. What have we done but play our part?'

Epilogue

The thing is, Alfonso, you and I may spend time in prison, you and I may eventually wither away in there. As the system says, we're too dangerous to be let back out. But I have immortality.

The papers will tell everyone what I created. They'll describe me as a monster, but over the years, people will see beyond that. They'll look at me and try to understand who I am, try to emulate me one day. When people talk about you, and keep talking about you, even though you're long gone, you live on. That's immortality, Alfonso. That's immortality.

They can take away my freedom, they can call me a monster, but they will acknowledge me. They'll forget the name Franz Kahn. Ron Boland and his camera work won't be there anymore. Young Sophie, now old Sophie, is already forgotten. But Stephen Fitz will be the name that lasts. It doesn't even matter that I didn't take his head, because they'll talk about the genius, how he understood me. It will come back to be about me. I have what I wanted. Immortality, Alfonso. Immortality. The greatest thing you can get from an excellent picture.

Read on to discover the Patrick Smythe series!

THE
WOMAN ON
THE MARINA
A PATRICK SMYTHE
MYSTERY THRILLER
G R JORDAN

Patrick Smythe is a former Northern Irish policeman who after suffering an amputation after a bomb blast, takes to the sea between the west coast of Scotland and his homeland to ply his trade as a private investigator. Join Paddy as he tries to work to his own ethics while knowing how to bend the rules he once enforced. Working from his beloved motorboat 'Craigantlet', Paddy decides to rescue a drug mule in this short story from the pen of G R Jordan.

Join G R Jordan's monthly newsletter about forthcoming releases and special writings for his tribe of avid readers and then receive your free Patrick Smythe short story.

Go to https://bit.ly/PatrickSmythe for your Patrick Smythe journey to start!

About the Author

GR Jordan is a self-published author who finally decided at forty that in order to have an enjoyable lifestyle, his creative beast within would have to be unleashed. His books mirror that conflict in life where acts of decency contend with self-promotion, goodness stares in horror at evil, and kindness blindsides us when we at our worst. Corrupting our world with his parade of wondrous and horrific characters, he highlights everyday tensions with fresh eyes whilst taking his methodical, intelligent mainstays on a roller-coaster ride of dilemmas, all the while suffering the banter of their provocative sidekicks.

A graduate of Loughborough University where he masqueraded as a chemical engineer but ultimately played American football, Gary had worked at changing the shape of cereal flakes and pulled a pallet truck for a living. Watching vegetables freeze at -40'C was another career highlight and he was also one of the Scottish Highlands "blind" air traffic controllers.

These days he has graduated to answering a telephone to people in trouble before telephoning other people to sort it out.

Having flirted with most places in the UK, he is now based in the Isle of Lewis in Scotland where his free time is spent between raising a young family with his wife, writing, figuring out how to work a loom and caring for a small flock of chickens. Luckily, his writing is influenced by his varied work and life experience as the chickens have not been the poetical inspiration he had hoped for!

You can connect with me on:

https://grjordan.com

https://facebook.com/carpetlessleprechaun

Subscribe to my newsletter:

https://bit.ly/PatrickSmythe

Also by G R Jordan

G R Jordan writes across multiple genres including crime, dark and action adventure fantasy, feel good fantasy, mystery thriller and horror fantasy. Below is a selection of his work. Whilst all books are available across online stores, signed copies are available at his personal shop.

Boomtown (Highlands & Islands Detective Book 35)

https://grjordan.com/product/boomtown

A series of explosions rock the Highlands and Islands. A population in panic as there seems no logic to the targets. Can Macleod and McGrath find the bomber in their midst before a promised massacre comes to fruition?

A seemingly accidental death caused by an explosion is the forerunner to a campaign of terror with an unknown purpose. As the incidents of unexplained eruptions continue, can DI Hope McGrath and DCI Macleod pool all their resources to discover what is behind the silent campaign of terror sweeping the North of Scotland?

The quieter the silence before, the bigger the bang after!

Kirsten Stewart Thrillers

https://grjordan.com/product/a-shot-at-democracy

Join Kirsten Stewart on a shadowy ride through the underbelly of the Highlands of Scotland where among the beauty and splendour of the majestic landscape lies corruption and intrigue to match any city. From murders to extortion, missing children to criminals operating above the law, the Highland former detective must learn a tougher edge to her work as she puts her own life on the line to protect those who cannot defend themselves.

Having left her beloved murder investigation team far behind, Kirsten has to battle personal tragedy and loss while adapting to a whole new way of executing her duties where your mistakes are your own. As Kirsten comes to terms with working with the new team, she often operates as the groups solo field agent, placing herself in danger and trouble to rescue those caught on the dark side of life. With action packed scenes and tense scenarios of murder and greed, the Kirsten Stewart thrillers will have you turning page after page to see your favourite Scottish lass home!

There's life after Macleod, but a whole new world of death!

Jac's Revenge (A Jack Moonshine Thriller #1)
https://grjordan.com/product/jacs-revenge
An unexpected hit makes Debbie a widow. The attention of her man's killer spawns a brutal yet classy alter ego. But how far can you play the game before it takes over your life?

All her life, Debbie Parlor lived in her man's shadow, knowing his work was never truly honest. She turned her head from news stories and rumours. But when he was disposed of for his smile to placate a rival crime lord, Jac Moonshine was born. And when Debbie is paid compensation for her loss like her car was written off, Jac decides that enough is enough.

Get on board with this tongue-in-cheek revenge thriller that will make you question how far you would go to avenge a loved one, and how much you would enjoy it!

A Giant Killing (Siobhan Duffy Mysteries #1)
https://grjordan.com/product/a-giant-killing

A body lies on the Giant's boot. Discord, as the master of secrets has been found. Can former spy Siobhan Duffy find the killer before they execute her former colleagues?

When retired operative Siobhan Duffy sees the killing of her former master in the paper, her unease sends her down a path of discovery and fear. Aided by her young housekeeper and scruff of a gardener, Siobhan begins a quest to discover the reason for her spy boss' death and unravels a can of worms today's masters would rather keep closed. But in a world of secrets, the difference between revenge and simple, if brutal, housekeeping becomes the hardest truth to know.

The past is a child who never leaves home!

Milton Keynes UK
Ingram Content Group UK Ltd.
UKHW041628240924
448733UK00002B/36

9 781915 562906